The Cl
from the First Age

Stories selected from issues 1-10 of
award winning
Shoreline of Infinity Science Fiction Magazine

Edited by Noel Chidwick

Shoreline *of* Infinity
Publications

To you
who
encouraged, supported and cheered us along.

The Chosen from the First Age

Stories selected from issues 1-10 of
award winning
Shoreline of Infinity Science Fiction Magazine

Edited by Noel Chidwick

ISBN 978-1-9993331-1-9

www.shorelineofinfinity.com

Publisher
Shoreline of Infinity Publications/The New Curiosity Shop
Edinburgh
Scotland
Typesetting and layout by The New Curiosity Shop

Shoreline of Infinity Publications, The New Curiosity Shop
and Noel Chidwick are members of the Shoreline of Infinity Group

www.shorelineofinfinity.com

040219

Cover: Stephen Pickering

Contents

Shoreline of Infinity
Science Fiction Magazine
Editorial Team

Co-founder, Editor-in-Chief& Editor:
Noel Chidwick

Co-founder, Art Director:
Mark Toner

Deputy Editor & Poetry Editor:
Russell Jones

Reviews Editor:
Samantha Dolan

Assistant Editor & First Reader:
Monica Burns

Copy editors:
Iain Maloney, Russell Jones, Monica
Burns, Pippa Goldschmidt

First Contact

www.shorelineofinfinity.com

contact@shorelineofInfinity.com

Twitter: @shoreinf

and on Facebook

**Shoreline of Infinity science
fiction magazine is available
from all good bookshops and
from our website
www.shorelineofinfinity.com
in paperback and digital
formats. For a discount code
skip to the last page.**

Pull Up a Log

After only three years in existence *Shoreline of Infinity Science Fiction Magazine* won the British Fantasy Society Award 2018 for best magazine/periodical.

To celebrate this fantastic honour we decided to publish a selection of stories from issues 1-10 (including a special edition 8½). The stories were chosen by the Shoreline team – the wonderful volunteers who have gathered around the Shoreline flames to make the magazine and our other Shoreline projects happen.

At events I'm often asked to recommend an issue – nope: I can't do that. Like children, I love 'em all; no favourites. The same goes for this collection – we almost picked every story.

Instead, we aimed for representation.

These stories are chosen as together they are the ambassadors for the magazine; together, we felt, they represent the character of the magazine – welcoming, challenging, enthralling, maybe a touch mischievous. If these stories were folk you were meeting in a bar, or a coffee shop, or indeed gathered around the camp-fire on the sands, you'd enjoy their diverse conversations.

And that's what I feel makes Shoreline of Infinity special. It's a gathering from all corners, where we all have a keen interest in exploring and understanding worlds near and far and the inhabitants therein.

Pull up a log and make yourself comfortable. Turn the page and meet *The Stilt-Men of the Lunar Swamps*.

—*Noel Chidwick, Editor-in-Chief*
Shoreline of Infinity
February 2019

The Stilt-Men of the Lunar Swamps

Andrew J. Wilson

I. Introductions Are Made

The yarn I'm about to tell you had almost spun itself out by the time I picked up the thread. Still, I was very lucky to have heard it at all, and in the end, I too got to play a small part in the story of the stilt-men of the lunar swamps.

I was enjoying a nightcap in the faded splendour of New York City's Weckquaesgeek Hotel when a garrulous drunk drew my attention. The red-faced man trying to cadge yet more liquor from the other patrons of the bar was, I realised, none other than Donald "Bud" Franklin. His slurred words grew louder as his temper flared, and it became clear that the Korean War veteran and former lunar astronaut was about to make a scene. Franklin climbed unsteadily onto a table, then bent over and dropped his trousers, shouting, "Here's two moons for the price of one, ya goddam rubberneckers!"

He'd been caught in a downward spiral since leaving the Apollo programme, and had finally reduced himself to the level of a side-show freak. But this was only the beginning of Big Bad Bud's performance, and his audience were in for much more than they'd bargained for that evening.

"Now," he yelled between his legs, "since y'all are so interested in what it was like, I'll give ya a practical demonstration of a Saturn V launch!" Then he waved a Zippo lighter around his buttocks and broke wind.

In the ensuing chaos, I spotted a small and elegant old woman who remained unperturbed. There was something familiar about her wrinkled face, as well as the way she calmly smoked pastel-coloured Balkan Sobranies in a stylish cigarette holder. When she realised that I'd been watching her, she beckoned me over to her table.

"Did you know that GI Bud Franklin is an anagram of 'blinking fraud'?" Her pleasantly raspy voice and inimitable turn of phrase told me who she was.

"Madam, I'm honoured," I said.

"But you *had* assumed I was dead, yes?"

She was, as ever, quite correct.

"Don't concern yourself, young man. Even I have to scan the obituaries every morning to reassure myself that I'm still in the land of the living."

Ursula Underhill was one of the greatest wits and finest literary stylists of her generation. I was so pleased to be in her presence that I'd almost completely forgotten about Franklin's idiocy until the security guards blundered past us, the former astronaut and his abandoned trousers clamped firmly in their sweaty hands.

"It's tragic, really," Ursula sighed, "but then the poor soul never saw the real Moon. Perhaps things might have been different if he had."

"I beg your pardon?"

"Oh, I was there years before all that NASA hoo-hah."

I stared at her in consternation, worried that she might be rambling with senility – and taken aback by her pronunciation of the acronym of the National Aeronautics and Space Administration as "Nassau".

"Don't look at me like that, young man… otherwise, I won't give you the story of a lifetime!"

II. The Professor's Exposition

You see, young man, even for a woman of my meagre talents, it was something of a disappointment to be relegated to the role of gossip columnist. I had arrived in England determined to make my mark as a social and political commentator. However, I rapidly found that all I could place were trivial sketches of the idle and the vain. These were times when men were men, and quite frankly, my dear, women were appalled.

You're too young to have heard of Montgomery Montgolfier Monk, big game hunter, self-styled adventurer and would-be lady killer. His monogram was MMM, and he insisted that it should be pronounced "mmm". The oaf thought it charming to whisper in the shell-like ears of debutantes that he was just a big sweetie, hard on the outside but soft within. Soft in the head was more like it, and I found his syrupy sayings more sickly than sweet. He was the kind of man who put the "ass" in passion.

Still, Monty Monk must have decided that I was a challenge to be scaled like one of his mountains, or bagged like some poor beast of the jungle. He fed me titbits for my columns, and introduced me to the eccentric orbit of a gang of socialites who were, Lord help me, even ghastlier and more ridiculous than him. I tolerated his persistence, and he eventually introduced me to his godfather, Professor Festus MacGuffin.

It must have been late in the autumn of nineteen thirty-two when Monty drove me down to the professor's estate in Berkshire. He had spun me a line about a great news story, and obviously thought he was going to be able to hook me with this so-called scoop and then reel me in over the course of the weekend. I was very much on my guard for the whole journey, but as we drove through the heavily wooded grounds, I realised that Triple-M might have inadvertently made my career.

Standing on the lawns screened by the trees was what I can only describe as an enormous steel sieve. I could not imagine the purpose of such an eyesore, but Monty assured me that it would be the sensation of the age before making it obvious that he had no idea what it was either.

We were met at the door by a neat young Oriental, whom Monty introduced as Kong.

"The professor is expecting you," the Chinaman told us with hardly a trace of any accent. "Dinner will be at eight, and your host will be pleased to demonstrate his latest invention immediately afterwards."

MacGuffin was one of the last surviving gentleman scientists, that enthusiastic species of amateur investigator who had flourished in the Victorian age. Now in his seventies, he combined bookish erudition with the manners of a country squire. His patriarchal beard was so bushy it looked as if he had tried to swallow a baby badger, but failed miserably in the attempt.

"Y'see, m'dear," he told me over the roast pheasant, "I've cracked the problem at last – I can now remotely observe the farthest parts of the world, all from the comfort of m'own study, don't y'know! The

Omniscope is a window on the world, and perhaps on other spheres as well…"

By the time the men were on to the port and cigars, I had listened to a barely coherent monologue about the technical details, which had gone over my head, out the door and all the way to Timbuktu. Monty had revelled in every word, but by the vacant look on his face, he had made even less sense of it than myself. The boob was simply taking childish delight in the sound of big words like 'selenography' and 'phlogiston'. Even the professor seemed to lose his thread half the time, and was compelled to ask Kong for clarification as the taciturn Oriental waited on us.

The Chinaman's moustache hung like quotation marks around the proverbially inscrutable slash of his mouth as he murmured definitions or ironed out details. Not only was Kong master chef, *maître d'* and chief bottle-washer for MacGuffin, I began to suspect that he was also quite probably the man who had built the Omniscope too.

"Come on, godparent, let's see the bally thing in action then!" Monty said at last, and we all trooped down the hall to the study.

A projection screen filled one whole wall. A veritable spaghetti Bolognese of wiring connected this apparatus to a brass control unit, which was, in turn, hooked up to the gigantic sieve on the other side of the partially open French windows.

"You do the honours, Kong," the professor said, and the whole lash-up was switched on. A wavering image came slowly into focus, and we realised that we were looking at ourselves.

"Have I put on weight?" bleated Monty as he saw himself from behind, but everyone else ignored him as Kong tweaked the controls. The screen blurred again and we saw London Bridge.

"The Taj Mahal next, I think!" the professor commanded, and so it was. People and places were paraded before us, and I, for one, was completely captivated by this novel magic lantern show. Unfortunately, Monty had an attention span so short it couldn't form a bridge across the space between his ears.

"Seen it before, been there, done that," he rambled irritatingly after only a few minutes.

"Gadzooks, lad! Are y'tired of the grand tour already?" the professor retorted and turned to his assistant. "Go on, Kong, pull out all the stops!"

The picture was wiped blank in a trice and only a few spangles of light broke the velvety darkness. Then the Moon loomed into view like a great, mottled balloon. The perspective lurched sickeningly, and the grey face of the rocky ball swelled to fill the screen.

"It looks a little arid," I remarked dryly as the seas, craters and ridges of our satellite became ever larger and more detailed.

"Wait, m'dear," the professor cautioned. "Although this airless waste is the lunar surface, it's only one part of it…"

A vast and seemingly bottomless crater came into view. Then our viewpoint plunged into the darkened well, and the sides of the shadowy pit slipped past at extreme speed. Eventually, stars pinpricked the darkness at what I imagined should have been the bottom of the enormous shaft, and I was amazed to find that the tunnel ran right through the core of our satellite.

"Now we'll be the first people to see the dark side of the Moon," the professor crowed with glee. "Then to the lunar pole, Kong!"

More drab and lifeless territory flashed past until we were confronted by a gigantic ice-ringed pit that punctured the roof of the Moon. For a moment, as if by pre-arrangement, the vertiginous motion ceased and Kong took his hands from the controls of the Omniscope. The professor lit his pipe as I struggled to catch up with my shorthand notes, then he addressed the room.

"Dear lady and gentlemen, not only have we proved the worth of the Omniscope, I've accomplished the main task for which it was designed!" Kong applauded politely as Monty and I glanced at each other in confusion. "Many astronomers have recently maintained that the Moon is a barren desert with no atmosphere worth speaking of – a celestial Slough, if you will. Their understandable error has been founded on astronomical observations of only one part of the lunar exterior. They would say one half of the surface, but I now argue that their telescopes can view even less. For, y'see, the Moon is a Klein bottle – a Möbius strip spun into three dimensions – a satellite with a single surface that can be exposed to vacuum on what previous observers have mistakenly described as its 'outside', but one that may sustain an entirely different environment within!"

My astonishment at what had gone before was made redundant by what happened next. Kong manipulated the levers, and our perspective plummeted into the vast hole yawning in the pockmarked surface. Far from the Stygian tunnel that we had observed previously, we were shown a realm of cloudy luminescence as our bird's-eye view drifted into the hidden realm.

"Just as I thought, m'boy!" the professor chortled as he nudged the dazed-looking Monty into alertness again. "The Moon does have an atmosphere – on the inside! And there's light too. Any thoughts, Kong?"

"I would hazard a guess that phosphorescence from minerals, or even rudimentary life forms, could be responsible for the illumination we can see, Professor," his assistant replied.

"Rudimentary?" I asked incredulously as the cloud cover broke and an extraordinary landscape became visible. Life burgeoned within the Moon: corkscrew trees with indigo foliage erupted from a swamp that steamed like primordial soup; things with leathery wings swooped over the forest snapping at iridescent insects of every shape and size; and down in the mire, massive eels coiled through the waters – or perhaps these were just the tentacles of some even more mind-boggling beast.

Wonder followed wonder in this subterranean bayou. Then we came upon the things that walked like men, but even more like men on stilts. Their extraordinarily long legs allowed these prodigies of nature to stride unhindered across the turbid waters of their world, while great flapping ears like those of elephants seemed to act as balancing mechanisms. In other respects, the creatures seemed almost human. They even wore simple, roughly made clothes, including huge puffy hats, and carried tools which looked surprisingly sophisticated.

"That one, Kong," the professor barked. "Let's take a closer look at this fellow and see what he's got in his three-fingered hands."

Monty had wandered right up to screen, as if mesmerised by the images. "It looks like he's got some kind of camera in his mitts. Golly, you can almost smell the swamp water... In fact, you can almost smell the blighter himself –"

Things became somewhat confused at this point.

As the Omniscope zeroed in on the stilt-man, the creature started in surprise, folded his face in a frown, and jerked the lens of his own contraption in what seemed to be our direction. There was a bang as several of the valves on the console exploded. Then, accompanied by an audible pop, the stilt-man reached *through* the screen and grabbed a flabbergasted Monty Monk by the ears. It was a moment's work for the Man-in-the-Moon to haul the man about town through the window made by the Omniscope – and into the strange new world on the other side.

At this point, the power failed and the professor's study was plunged into darkness. Three things were audible: Monty's fading squeals of "Oh, I say!"; the professor's inventive but unprintable profanity; and someone or something yelling, "Kumquats! Hose-pipe! Banana peel!"

III. A Surprising Development

As soon as the lights had flickered on again, Kong set about repairing what I now regarded as *his* machine. Once the spent valves were replaced, the view of the now-deserted lunar swamps came back into focus. The professor repeatedly poked a shooting stick through the Omniscope's screen to confirm that the weird portal remained open, and we hatched a Curate's egg of a plan.

MacGuffin gathered together the rest of his staff and assembled an arsenal of small arms and hunting rifles. The French windows were opened wide, and the servants hauled a small motor launch – commandeered from a nearby lake – along the drive, through the study and up to the screen, before plunging it into the waters of the lunar interior. Finally, Kong, the professor and I – all now changed into outdoor clothing – clambered through the omniscopic window and into the boat. The lower lunar gravity made the transition difficult, but reassuringly increased our strength in that curious place.

Looking back at our point of entry, I was disoriented by the sight of the portal hanging in mid-air. It was as if a magical knife had cut a rectangular hole in reality, peeling away a slice of the lunar landscape to reveal the professor's crowded study. One could even have fancied that the scene was only a cleverly rendered *trompe-l'œil*, if not for the busy movements of the servants within. Queerer still was the effect created when Kong piloted our boat around the portal, for there was no back to the gateway! We found that our egress only existed in one dimension: there was no discernible edge to the thing, and our views of the steaming lunar interior were uninterrupted once we had positioned ourselves to the rear.

Such riddles could have occupied us for days, but that was time we could ill afford to spend in contemplation when we had a blue-blooded buffoon to rescue. Kong gunned the engine and the launch surged forward, taking us towards our unsolicited appointment with destiny.

It was only once we were moving that the professor remembered that I was a woman.

"Good God, we can't take you with us, gel – this is no place for a lady. Kong, turn this boat around!"

I was about to argue when Kong replied for me.

"I believe that Miss Underhill was one of the leading markswomen in the ladies' shooting club when she attended Harvard, sir."

MacGuffin stared at me as I nodded frostily, adding, "One doesn't like to boast." The matter was settled when I pointedly plucked a large log from the water and crushed it with my bare hands. "What's more, I no longer appear to be a member of the weaker sex in this sphere."

Kong steered the boat in a broad circle through the mauve and heliotrope foliage. The purplish world around us exploded with life as we passed. Most of the bizarre creatures around us fled from the noise, fumes and surging wake of our boat, and the rest recoiled from sharp blows from the professor's shooting stick.

The air was heavy with humidity and the overpoweringly spicy odours of the swamp. High above us, thick cumuli boiled around a nebulous source of light. Some of these clouds seemed to break apart into smaller clumps, and these floated downwards in a distinct direction. Although we saw no stilt-men, the drifting clouds pointed us towards what had to be their stronghold.

A great spiral tower rose out of the swamps, beckoning us like an index finger signalling to a lackadaisical waiter. We certainly intended to give the Moon-men something to chew on, but I, for one, was not out to serve up any dish as cold as revenge. Rather, I wanted to spare the stilt-men from sampling too much of their entrée – Monty Monk was hardly a good appetiser for our civilisation. To be frank, he was enough to give anybody indigestion.

"We'll give 'em Hell for kidnapping m'godson, won't we, m'dear?" MacGuffin growled. "Two crack shots should be enough to settle their hash. Course Kong here won't touch firearms because of his religion, but he's a master of Carrot or Judy, one of those Oriental martial arts."

"With all due respect, I think we should be careful, Professor," I replied. "After all, the stilt-man may have just been as curious as we were. We don't know he meant any harm."

"Well, he acted as if he was up to no good – I say we take no chances, no prisoners and no lip!"

"If I may, Professor," Kong interjected, "let me agree with Miss Underhill's suggestion that we employ a modicum of caution in our dealings with these creatures."

"Why, man? Tell me why we should give these savages anything more than the hiding they deserve."

Kong visibly held his tongue for a moment, then composed himself before continuing.

"Because, Professor, they can hardly be counted as savages…"

MacGuffin snorted like a surfacing walrus.

"Balderdash, man, how else would you describe the beggars?"

"I wouldn't care to hazard a guess without further data, sir, but one thing is certainly clear – they're advanced enough to have developed their own equivalent of the Omniscope."

"Hogwash!"

"That can be the only explanation for our present predicament. You will remember that the creature who took Mister Monk was using a device when we first caught sight of him, a device he turned in our direction…"

I did indeed recall the camera-like apparatus that the stilt-man had been operating, as did the professor, if his wordless grumble was anything to go by.

"I surmise that it has to be a mechanism very like our own. That can be the only explanation for the tear in the fabric of space. We observed him as he turned his own Omniscope in our direction and the beams of the two devices interfered with each other, creating the disruption that has bridged the gap between our two worlds…"

"Oh," said the professor succinctly before qualifying this pearl of wisdom with a superfluous, "Ah."

The debate was obviously at an end.

Kong sent the launch hurtling into a broad channel lined with the corkscrew trees. It seemed to lead straight to the cyclopean tower.

"Let us all be on our guard," he warned as we cocked our weapons.

Then some of the tree trunks moved in the water, and I realised that we were surrounded by hooting stilt-men who had hidden their upper bodies in the thick foliage.

"Hell's teeth!" the professor bellowed, but their nets were upon us as he cried out. Our launch remained spinning in the water as we were hauled upwards in the sticky mesh. Even though we were hoisted by our own petard, we were well and truly sunk.

IV. Capitulation And Recapitulation

I have no memory of swooning, but I will never forget recovering consciousness at the top of that improbable tower. My self-disgust at passing out like the simpering heroine of dime-novel cliché was allayed by the realisation that both Kong and the professor were also recovering from fainting spells. I concluded fuzzily that we had all been drugged. Our guns were gone, but someone had had sufficient decency to leave me with my handbag. Then I managed to focus on my surroundings and was greeted by the nauseating sight of a nearly naked Monty Monk wearing what looked like a giant turban and holding hands with similarly attired stilt-men.

"Quisling quack-quack blancmange," Monty announced.

"Toad snipe, toad snipe!" one of the Moon-men snapped, and Monty adjusted his strange headgear.

"Ah, hello? Oh yes, much better! Evening all!"

"What in the blue blazes is going on, dear boy?" the professor demanded. "What have these lanky fiends done to you?"

Monty laughed with a peculiarly girlish giggle. "I'm in the club! I've become a member of the lunar élite." We looked at him as if he had lost the last of the few wits that God had given him. "The tall chaps are just servants around here, you see – it's the floaty fellows on our heads who are *la crème de la crème* around here." The strange hats did indeed look like swollen brains, and I realised with a shock that the clouds we had seen scudding towards the tower had actually been these curious lumps of grey matter.

"Long, long ago," Monty went on, "before their ancestors came down from the stars and colonised the interior of the Moon, they were all the same. Then evolution took over. The menials who did the work stayed on the ground, growing ever longer legs to get around the swamps, while the nobility simply evolved into a more gaseous form of lighter-than-air being that could float free and enjoy the high life. Nowadays, the élite either sun themselves around the lodestone that holds the air in and lights up the place, or pop down, sit on people's

16

heads and tell their minions what do. It's absolutely super! They want me to be part of it – and you too –"

"Now, Monty," I said, "no one ever pretended that you were the sharpest blade in the shaving kit, but presumably, since you haven't yet learned to fly, this would mean that they want you to be one of their slaves too."

"Would it?" Monty asked before adjusting the brain-beast squatting on his head, as if he was tuning the cat's whisker of a wireless set. "Oh, right, yes – it would."

"Beatle wig, sandwich board, fondue," one of the stilt-men ordered sternly while pointing at the three of us with a sucker-tipped finger. We were hauled to our feet and dragged towards a ledge like a gangplank at the edge of the tower. Three floating brains drifted towards us with menacing intent, their eyestalks and vestigial limbs wriggling greedily.

"Montgomery Montgolfier Monk, you are a disgrace to your country and the Crown!" Professor MacGuffin said with disgust. "You may be quite content to wander about naked as the day you were born wearing a power-crazed tea-cosy on your head, but I, sir, am certainly *not* of that kidney!" The professor struggled, but even under the lesser lunar gravity, he could not shake off his captors. "I am prepared to fight the mesmeric might of these malevolent mentalists with my own will, but spare the lesser fortitude of the woman and my servant –"

Kong turned his placid and inscrutable face to me, and whispered a few words of comfort: "Madam, as I believe Confucius himself once said, 'Sod this for a game of soldiers!'"

He moved with startling grace, catching his captors off balance and flinging them bodily into the guards holding me. Then the Chinaman's hands and feet moved with uncanny speed in the reduced gravity, chopping and kicking this way and that. The spindly guards were sent flying and we were free for a moment, but more of the puppet-like stilt-men were already charging up the stairs to seize us.

"Miss Underhill," Kong cried, even as he was brought down and gagged, "your cigarette lighter –"

It seemed odd that any man should suggest that a woman should commit the social *faux pas* of smoking outside, even at a time like this. However, as one of the floating monsters reared above me, I guessed what he meant. If the things were lighter than air, then they had to contain pockets of gas like a Zeppelin – gas that was probably combustible.

In a trice, I pulled my lighter from my bag and struck the flint. The brain-beast veered, but I tickled its underside with the naked flame.

There was ghastly, flatulent bang and the ugly lump of grey matter shot off like a skyrocket before exploding messily in mid-air. Everyone else froze for a moment. I advanced on the other creatures, all perched like substandard millinery on the stilt-men's heads, and the rout began.

The humid and watery environment of the lunar interior had meant that fire, the Achilles' heel of the floating dictators, had never troubled them before. Once some of the stilt-men had been released from their mental bondage, their minds soon cleared, and they helped us to liberate more of their kind. All-out revolution was in progress around the tower before long. Freedom spread – and I choose my words with care – like wildfire. The brain-beasts knew they were toast and fled for the skies, floating dejectedly away from the lands they had ruled so poorly.

We returned to our launch escorted by a host of joyful stilt-men.

"Parsnip! Parsnip!" they cried gratefully as we cast off, but the comment was lost on us. We tried to be polite by randomly shouting the names of other root vegetables back at them.

We returned to the Omniscope portal uneventfully, and were pleasantly surprised to re-enter the world we knew in time for breakfast.

V. Coda In Codicil

"So you see, I *was* on the Moon," Ursula Underhill concluded with a twinkle in her eye.

I stared at her, quite lost for words. "Oh, don't concern yourself, young man, I didn't expect you to believe me. Now, could you take my bag and escort me to my room? I am weary and must retire."

As I took Ursula by the arm and helped her to the elevator, I finally found my voice.

"Why did you never tell anyone before?"

"Well, that was the first thing Monty did. They put him in the booby hatch for a couple of years before he learnt to keep his trap shut."

"What about the professor?"

"Oh, he wanted to hush it all up. I had worked out that Kong was responsible for most of the actual work, and the old fool was ashamed that he had taken credit for another man's work – a Chinaman's creation at that. The 'professor' title was also a sore point. I don't believe he'd ever attended a university, let alone taught at one…"

"And the redoubtable Kong?"

"Well, I don't know much about the martial arts, but I can assure you that he was very accomplished at the marital ones. We were wed the following spring, you see."

We reached her room and I helped her to a cushioned chair. Ursula asked me to open her bag and place its contents on the dressing table.

"A gift from my late husband," she told me.

I found a curious box, not unlike a manual typewriter, with brass controls and some kind of projector.

"I'm so old, my dear," she said sadly. "My bones are brittle and all my friends have gone. I'm not long for this world, you know."

"It's been an honour," I said, and left her to her thoughts.

Then a strange thing happened in the hallway. I heard a pop, saw a purple flash, and then someone or something clearly said, "Semolina trouser press."

Ursula Underhill's door swung open and, concerned, I went back in, but there was no one there and the curious gift from Kong had gone too. Outside the window, a full moon hung over the New York skyline.

I bowed politely in its direction, saying, "Parsnip, parsnip," before I left the room again and gently closed the door.

Andrew J. Wilson is a freelance editor and writer. His short stories, non-fiction and poems have appeared all over the world, sometimes in the most unlikely places. With Neil Williamson, he co-edited *Nova Scotia: New Scottish Speculative Fiction*, which was nominated for a World Fantasy Award.

See You Later
M Luke McDonell

Arabella's front door beeped in polite disapproval of her polymer-coated iris. Hurriedly, she typed in the long access code and held her palm to the scanner, but too late. Mrs. Constantino was out of her apartment and shuffling down the hall towards her, the frayed hems of her oversized sweat pants dragging on the clean white carpet.

"Something wrong, honey? Lock stuck? I've been having the same trouble with my windows. I called the management company but all they do is send a reset code that doesn't fix anything."

Arabella breathed through her mouth to avoid the smells of vodka and cat pee that blanketed the old woman. All the residents complained that they'd moved into this building to get away from the riffraff on the streets and now they had to deal with it in the halls. Mrs. Constantino was somehow able to afford the sky-high rent though, so there was nothing to be done about her.

The lock retracted but Arabella held the door shut. Mrs. Constantino was oblivious to polite hints and would stay for hours if she let her in.

"You okay, honey? You been crying?" Mrs. Constantino asked.

Arabella resisted the urge to rub her aching eyes. The technician warned her not to touch them for 24 hours. "No, I just got AR lenses."

Mrs. Constantino's wrinkled face lit up in a smile. "You're going to love them. I can see better than a hawk now."

Arabella forced herself to examine Mrs. Constantino's bloodshot eyes and indeed, a thin silver line traced the iris. Where *did* this woman get her money? "I didn't need them for medical reasons," she admitted. "I have 20/10 vision now."

Mrs. Constantino winked. "You don't have to tell me these are more than fancy glasses."

As she drew in a burbling breath to elaborate, Arabella pushed the door open and slipped inside. "I'm supposed to rest," she called in weak apology as she slammed the door behind her.

In the bathroom, she stared at the silver ring of her iris with distaste. The irony was that Hugh hadn't wanted the lenses either. He treated his body like a rare sports car, too precious to drive. When his company insisted that all senior management get the permanent implants – a bleeding-edge technology not yet legal in the EU – he actually considered quitting.

Arabella rarely put her foot down but in this case she did so with force. Her husband's last promotion was contingent on a move to this decrepit city – one of the last outposts of cheap labor. She'd had to leave her friends, her favorite sushi restaurant, and the hairdresser she'd finally trained to give her a proper cut. Hugh would damn well get some plastic in his eye after all the sacrifices she'd made.

She'd grown to regret her insistence. Hugh had become increasingly distant in the months since he'd gotten the implants. He came home from work earlier, but shushed her when she tried to speak to him.

"I'm in a meeting," he'd say, exasperated, waving his hand to indicate a conference table she couldn't see. He moved through the apartment in strange patterns, avoiding things that weren't there and clipping the edges of furniture that was.

He wouldn't watch streams with her on the wall anymore, declaring the resolution inferior to what his eye screens displayed. In theory, they could view the same content simultaneously and Hugh made a show of synching his glasses with the wall, but when he sat next to her, head tilted to the ceiling, giggling during the tense parts of dramas, she knew he was seeing something else.

They'd had plenty of bumps on the road of marriage before, but at least they'd been looking out the same windshield. She would fix this.

Arabella ran icy cold water over her face until the pain in her eyes subsided. She had to hurry. Hugh would be home from work soon. He didn't know she was getting lenses, so hadn't bothered to lock the settings he'd spent months perfecting.

She approached the strange contraption in his office hesitantly. The black goggles, mounted on a thick silver pole, resembled a grotesque Venetian *carnevale* mask, wires instead of ribbons trailing from both edges. The technician had explained that the tiny screens needed to be recharged once a day and that was a good time to adjust settings as well. Contrast, brightness, automatic data overlays – Arabella had only half-listened to the detailed instructions. She'd use Hugh's settings; that was the point of getting these, after all.

She leaned in. Tiny white words appeared in the darkness. *Recharge?* in the center, *Yes* and *No*, on the far left and right respectively, appeared beneath.

Arabella gazed steadily at *Yes*.

A green circle appeared. Watch the dot for the next 15 seconds. Please do not blink, the text directed.

So far, so good. After the elapsed time, another menu appeared. *Update settings?* And beneath, *Home, Work,* and *New.*

She selected *Home* and held still as information was transferred to the tiny processors.

Your update is complete.

Arabella straightened, blinking rapidly in the suddenly too-bright light. What was this? The view from the upper-floor window was no longer of polluted Lake Tanganyika but of a busy, beachfront promenade. Bikini-clad teen girls, pale, sweaty tourists, and overly-tanned men in linen suits paraded past a backdrop of white sand and turquoise sea.

It took her a moment to recognize this was Ocean Drive in Miami. She'd accompanied Hugh to a conference in South Beach last year. They'd both found the city incredibly gauche and the newly-passed ordinance allowing nude sunbathing was ridiculous and unsanitary.

Yet, here she was. The resolution was incredible. A teen girl, modestly clad in a thong bikini, retrieved a volleyball from the footpath and raced back to her game. Sunlight glinted off the rhinestones of a passing woman's purse and cast rainbows on the ceiling of the room. Arabella reached to remove her glasses – her usual method of consuming virtual reality – before remembering she wasn't wearing any.

Turning her back on the glare of the window, she was confronted by a Fauvist interpretation of the muted impressionist color palette she'd used to decorate Hugh's office. One wall was acid yellow, the others, bright orange.

The living room was even worse. The elegant Louis XIV furniture she'd spent a fortune to ship from London was now a collection of blocky, modernist eyesores. A simple, square light fixture replaced the beautiful cut crystal chandelier she'd won at auction. Had Hugh lost his mind?

Eyes aching from this onslaught, she returned to the bathroom to again splash her face, but, where was it? Not the bathroom – thankfully Hugh hadn't changed anything there – but her face? This was a real mirror, not a screen, and she stared straight through herself to the spectrum of beige towels on the wall behind her. She held up her hands – nothing.

Oh god, she'd gotten a bad pair of lenses. This was why the EU hadn't approved them yet. Was it too late to get them removed? The nanobots needed 24 hours to bond with her eye tissue.

Back in the office, she tried to find the troubleshooting guide on the charging station but the menus cascaded into infinity. She needed help.

Mrs. Constantino answered the door so quickly she must have been standing beside it.

"I'm so sorry," Arabella began, but Mrs. Constantino needed no explanation.

"Come in, dear."

She ushered Arabella into a large, clean living room. Framed photographs of buildings covered the six-meter high walls.

Arabella gaped. "I didn't know any of the apartments had such high ceilings."

Mrs. Constantino smiled. "My husband was a builder. *The* builder, in this case. He gave us the best unit. Would you like a tour?"

Arabella contemplated her invisible feet. "Maybe later. Right now I need help resetting my lenses. Something is wrong."

Mrs. Constantino crooked a finger. "Come to my room. We'll fix you up."

Her bedroom was as neat and tasteful as the living room. Arabella couldn't reconcile this walking pile of rags with the upscale furniture that surrounded her, and the cats she was sure infested the place had yet to make an appearance.

Mrs. Constantino gestured to a rig similar to Hugh's. "Lean in and I'll talk you through it."

A few minutes later, Arabella hurried to a large white and gold mirror and looked with relief into her own red-veined eyes. "Thank you so much. I downloaded my husband's settings and..."

Mrs. Constantino shushed her and took her arm. "Let's have a drink."

"Oh no, I–"

"I insist."

Arabella, surprised by the strength of the woman's grip, allowed herself to be led back to the living room. Mrs. Constantino mixed and poured two martinis with the ease of a hotel bartender.

"What was wrong with your lenses?" she asked, once she and Arabella were seated.

Arabella sipped tentatively. She usually drank white wine. "Well, the apartment was different, but that wasn't the real problem. I couldn't see myself!" She held out a slim, manicured hand. Still there.

Mrs. Constantino laughed, a disturbing half-cough, half-chortle. "Oh honey. Finish that drink and come here."

She swallowed hers in a gulp and waited for Arabella to choke down a bit more of the astringent liquid.

Back in the bedroom, Mrs. Constantino pointed to the charging station. "Get back on there. Choose 'Charles' from the settings menu. Don't worry, we'll put you back to basics after that."

Arabella did, hesitantly. Once her lenses were updated, she stepped back and faced a beautiful, lithe, 20 year-old woman with waist-length black hair.

The woman gazed at her with bewitching, long-lashed brown eyes. Smiling coquettishly, she turned slowly, showing off the kind of figure Arabella failed to attain despite hours a day at the gym.

"Your lenses aren't broken, honey," the beautiful woman proclaimed in an incongruously weary, feathery voice. "Your husband hasn't decided what you look like yet."

Arabella recalled the Miami beach scene, the garish colors in Hugh's office, the altered furniture in the living room, and her own invisibility.

"Unfortunately," she replied, "I'm afraid he has."

M. Luke McDonell's five-minutes-into-the-future fiction explores the effects of emerging technology on individuals and society. Her work has appeared in *Shoreline of Infinity, The Overcast, Perihelion*, and *New Reader Magazine*. By day, she is a senior designer at a San Francisco software security company and by night she writes and helps run internet radio station SomaFM.

Come along to Cymera, Scotland's first and only book festival celebrating Science Fiction, Fantasy and Horror Writing.

Meet local, national and international authors

Test your knowledge on our quiz

Entertain us with your work at our open mic

Submit to our writing competition

Dance the night away at our ceilidh

Feast your eyes on the works and publications in our creators' hall

Relish in the thrills of a Shoreline of Infinity's Event Horizon

Friday 7th June 2019 – Sunday 9th June

The Pleasance

Edinburgh

Full details and programme

www.cymerafestival.co.uk

Twitter: @CymeraF

I have never considered a companion – is that the word? – an organism to interact with. It has been such a lengthy duration and I was unaware of the existence of your kind – the existence of any of this – until relocated from Japeng Aquatic. Yes, the temperature is higher in Phototropi, but still humid. Throughout the last dyau-sequence I have been feeling my mass, which is new to me, and it weighs heavy. I am euryhaline but the first of mine to invert to terra. For genera I have laid immersed within the covalent bonds of Aquatic. Cold sodium chloride, then warmer habitats free of halite. Now I advance bipedally, neither one thing or the other. My new bones are durable. Microgravity activates the osteoclasts; they are fluorescent, quite mesmeric I once overheard, although I have never seen them myself as my retinas become

Model Organisms

Caroline Grebbell

Art: Sara Julia

weakened. You will view me as colourless, my
skin is dehydrated.

I was a model organism, as you were
Thaliana. There for the determination of genes,
toxicology, transgenic and haploid embryonic
stem cells. I was brought here to help them
learn. To assist them. That's what I believed.
That's what they told me. I was numerous at first
but have evolved to one. To this. I realise you are
aware of all I say, Thaliana, I tell you each time
we converse. I apologise, it is all I know, it is all
that is left for me to say but to say nothing for
want of something new is further suffering.

When did this split appear, this chasm
between spirit and physical worlds? How can
a spirit exist four-hundred kilometres above
its planet drowned? Anima? Your kind will
remember her.

I have been here the longest of durations.
I have spawned brood but they are from the
other, the Oryzias, the Meduka. They shifted me,
stretched me, twisted my form. They have lost
me and now I am losing you. Six dyau-sequence
is too short a duration for you to flourish. I
was permitted to observe you Thaliana, you
are exemplary. You may indeed be mesmeric.
The permission was a distraction I know, to
push reasoning from my solitude. But solitude
is not the focus of my reasoning. I exist more
humanoid than Oryzias now, my scales have
levelled, my surface lanulose, spermatozoa
multiplies in my ovaries. I am neither one thing
nor the other. From seed to germination I have
tended you Thaliana. You flowered then to seed

once more and now you are dying. To be pulled apart. Sectioned and evaluated. I too will be recalled for dissection but I am unknowing as to when. Unknowing as to what I will become. They have left me like this. My life ends and I do not know what I am.

And now we are to be separated. I am scared. I have seen so little. The True Aquatic was my home and then my jailer. I am lonely. We co-exist beneath the electro-rad of this artificial sunne. I fail to find even the remnants of a shadow in this habitat.

Should we ever wonder how it resulted in this, us and not the others, what did we show over them? Nothing perhaps. Nothing other than being plucked from the ether.

Do you live your memories? Ancient and distant but beyond my reach, they are duration-worn and strange, as if perhaps not my belonging at all. Perhaps they bind to the being I was before me or link to the me I am to become. An untroubled duration has been the one spent with you. And now you are dying. Your gestation is over, your span, and I am to be left alone. My bones are strong but my muscles grow stiff and rigid. I am lonely, Thaliana. I am atrophied and dying and they will watch me shrink and wither and turn their backs to continue their search. I am scared, Thaliana. Perhaps I will block my gills with your flowers and we can travel together.

Caroline Grebbell is a BSFA award nominated genre fiction writer and tv/film art director. She also makes comics and dabbles with the odd illustration. She doesn't crochet slippers for spiders.
www.carolinegrebbell.com

Shaker Loop

Bo Balder

Dad was demonstrating the disappearing drawers again. Patrick clung to his father's calf through the thick whipcord pants. A mist of one part irritation and two parts wonder descended on Patrick's uncles. Their stirring was a scary thing because their huge feet shuffled restlessly and asses got scratched, huge hands swinging down right past his face.

"Do it again, Paddy," his uncle Joe said.

"I got no keys to spare anymore," his dad said. "Anyone? Just gimme a matchbox or a cigarette, your keys are gonna be gone. Unless you don't believe me, of course."

"A waste of a good smoke," Uncle Riley said. His fingers, fidgeting with a freshly rolled cigarette, hung down next to Patrick's nose. His mom had recently issued a ban on smoking indoors. It didn't make the Christmas gathering any mellower.

"No one?" his dad said. "Joyce? Bring me a fork or something?"

"What? You want the good silver to disappear?" his mom yelled back.

"Here," Patrick said. He held out his prize possession, a purple and green Leatherhead figure from Teenage Mutant Ninja Turtles. If something made the keys disappear, he figured Leatherhead would know what to do with it. Anyway, he wasn't willing to risk Donatello or Leonardo.

"Hey, thanks, kid," dad said.

He held the figurine up for all the uncles to see.

Dad put Leatherhead in the left drawer. Not that it mattered, loose change and spare rubber bands disappeared from the right drawer just the same.

"You guys, look carefully. One toy. Everybody happy it's in there?"

"Yeah, yeah," Uncle Rod said. "You missed your calling, Pads, you should have joined the carnival after all."

Dad shoved the drawer shut with more force than necessary. "Okay, I'm gonna step back now. Roddy, you wanna do the honors?"

"What?" Uncle Joe said. "You just skip over your little brother? Nice going."

Patrick shoved his head against his dad's thighs. Not again. They had such loud voices, and with their big bellies and big hands they made the house seem so small. If it hadn't been snowing he'd have been in the treehouse looking over the lake. He was just like mom, or so dad said. Shy, bookish. Patrick wasn't sure that he was, he just didn't like his uncles always shouting and arguing and getting red in the face as the evening progressed.

"Hey!" Uncle Roddy said. "It's gone. How did you do that?"

He bent over and peered into the drawer, feeling inside it with his big hands. Patrick's dad intervened when Roddy threatened to yank the drawer from the casing.

"Hey, hey, careful, it's an heirloom."

"Doesn't mean it's yours," Uncle Roddy bit back. "You live here coz you're the eldest, but it's our house, too."

Uncle Joe intervened, as he always did. His father and uncles withdrew to the den to drink some more.

An heirloom. What did that mean? It was a shiny table from a kind of whirly wood. You couldn't play on it because there were no chairs allowed in the hall and anyway it was tiny. Grown-ups used it to put keys on or mail. But it did kind of get in the way of using the black-and-white tiles in the hallway for sliding. So all in all Patrick didn't think it was a very good piece of furniture. Maybe heirloom meant "kind of useless."

Patrick stood on tiptoes to check if Uncle Rod had been right. Yep, Leatherhead was gone. He opened the right drawer to check if the figurine was in there. All he found was a funny thing, like a tiny flat walkie-talkie. Only it was a gross, girly pink. And nothing happened if you pressed the buttons. He put it back. The right drawer only ever produced stuff like that, shiny, pretty, but pointless. If you put it back in, it disappeared.

His eyes prickled. Maybe he shouldn't have given Leatherhead away. He'd just wanted the uncles to stop wrangling. Mom was in the kitchen, grousing about making lunch for so many people. Better not to disturb her.

He went to his room to cuddle up with Leonardo and Donatello.

✳

When the last of the uncles had left, back to their normal lives, Patrick could breathe again. He climbed on the deep sills of the garden-side windows and closed the curtains behind him. It was dark outside, so he couldn't see anything, but it was safe and silent. No uncles to punch his arm or rough up his hair. The look on his dad's face meant he had to pretend to like that stuff, and that was the worst.

Mom yelled that dinner was ready. It would be warmed-up macaroni and cheese, his favorite. Dad took his plate outside to do some banging and swearing in the shed. He hung out with his brothers for the holiday duration and then he got mad he hadn't gotten around to fixing anything in grandpa's old workshop.

Patrick had proposed not inviting the uncles, but although mom had smiled at him, she'd also said they couldn't do that. "It's their house as much as ours, hon. We should be happy we get to live in it all the time."

Dad returned and played with the side table some more. Patrick didn't join him because he was tired of watching things disappear.

He slid off his chair to get in some reading time upstairs before Mom would make him turn off the light. Dad didn't want him to read during the day either, he should play outside like a little man.

As he crossed the hallway, dad grabbed his shoulder.

Patrick winced and tried to pull away. What had he done now?

But dad didn't box his ears or anything. He pulled him in against his oil and beer smelling shirt and mumbled something in his hair.

"What?" Patrick said.

"Nothing, buddy. Don't look so worried. You're my little guy, you know that, right?"

The only possible answer was yes.

Dad let him go. "Go read. It's fine."

Too surprised at this change of heart to answer, Patrick ran up the stairs to get to his book. He didn't want to waste any more good reading time.

※

Still reverberating from an unexpected divorce, Patrick returned to the lake house after his parents died. He just wanted to clear out some personal items and sell up the rest. Uncle Roddy and his family had dropped out of sight, and Patrick hadn't been able to locate his one cousin, Bee, Uncle Joe's daughter. The others had died before his dad.

He roamed through the emptying rooms as he triaged pieces for the bonfire or the yard sale, missing, strangely enough, the rowdy brothers and their fights. Six of them, full of vim and vigor, and now he was the only one of the next generation. And his own kids hadn't been allowed to come. His ex stuck to a rigid schedule of once a month, which the overly righteous judge had agreed to. He'd begged Allyson to lighten up just this once; they could see the old lake house, it had been in the family for generations…but no. No kids. Just him. Thirty-seven and counting.

He ran his hand over the old-fashioned wainscoting in the hallway. With his mother's rugs and knickknacks gone, it had regained some of its former grandeur. Those black and white tiles sure had been nice to glide on.

The Shaker sidetable was missing, like many of the old-looking pieces of furniture he remembered. His mother had never liked them – had she been selling them off over the years? Maybe it was in the shed.

The shed yielded up more burnable junk, but no sidetable. He wasn't sure why it mattered, he'd never thought about the thing in all those years.

He worked until late in the afternoon. The burnable pile was getting too high to toss more stuff on, but it seemed a waste of a good fire to light it by day. He loaded the sellable pieces into the truck. Driving through miles of bare trees, he rolled into the sleepy town, emptier than before, with more closed-up stores than he remembered. The antique cum junk cum loved-clothing store was still open.

Craig, the owner, still shock-haired although it had gone white, plucked his lower lip. "Some nice things in there, Paddy, but business isn't doing so great. Can't offer you much for it. How about a trade?"

Patrick laughed. "For what? I can't take stuff with me, I'm flying home after I sell this truck."

"I'll take the truck," Craig said. "Have a browse in my store. I'll give you more money's worth in trade than I can offer in cash."

God, that was sad. When he was a kid, it had felt like a happy, prosperous town, full of smiling people, so different from the grey frowns of Chicago townhouses.

"Okay," he said and followed Craig into the store.

And there it was. Amidst a jumble of incomplete china sets, stacked plastic chairs, football trophies, black and white TVs, art deco radio sets, mysterious chrome rods and other dusty, unappealing objects, stood the Shaker sidetable. Shinier, the wonky forepaw fixed with a pale synthetic, like a pony with a white fetlock. But it had somehow become prettier now, since Allyson had taught him about Shaker furniture in the intervening years.

"Where did you get that?"

"That's my white elephant. I keep having to buy it back because people complain about things disappearing and appearing in it." Craig looked as if he wished he'd kept his mouth shut.

"Huh. My parents used to own it, I think. Did my mom sell you this? "

"Before my time, I guess. You want it back? I'd be willing to include it in the trade," Craig said, a shade too eager.

Patrick scratched his head. Did he want the damn thing back? He didn't have any particularly important memories of it. He'd lost some kind of toy to it, which had sucked. Still.

He opened the left drawer.

And closed his hand possessively around Leatherhead. It couldn't be. But his hand knew it was the one he lost and didn't intend to let go. There was more in the drawer besides the figurine: a bunch of keys, a lighter, some change.

Patrick lifted the key label with his other hand. *3789 Wichita Rd.*, it said in his grandfather's shaky writing. It couldn't be. But here they were, all the objects that his dad and his uncles had tossed into the left drawer. He even smelled pine needles and rum. Christmas smells.

He put Leatherhead in his pocket, encountering something else in there. He fished it out. A broken cell phone from his daughter Hollis, forgotten in this ancient waxed coat, which he hardly ever used in the city.

He tossed it in the right drawer.

Right drawer goes back thirty years, left drawer goes forward thirty years, he mumbled to himself.

"You want it?" Craig asked.

Patrick startled. He'd forgotten all about the man and the stuff in his truck, the trade. But first he had to do something. Alone.

"Yeah," he said. "I do. You get started getting my stuff in here, I just need to do something."

Craig went.

He and his father had never seen eye to eye; he hadn't gone home more than once a year, if that, since college, and avoided talking to the old man as much as he could.

But the pain of separation from his own kids had made him wise to distant dads. They had feelings. Fathers did love, even if they sometimes couldn't show it much.

Patrick found a business card in his wallet, the one screaming in shonky purple characters: Associate Professor, Dept. Of English Literature, Northwestern.

"Dad, I love you," he wrote on the front. "From your son Patrick, December 2016."

He folded the scrap of paper, put it in the right drawer and shoved it shut before he could change his mind.

Bo Balder is the first Dutch author to have been published in *Clarkesworld* and *F&SF*. Her short fiction has also appeared in *Escape Pod, Nature* and other places. Her sf novel *The Wan* was published by Pink Narcissus Press.
Visit her website: www.boukjebalder.nl

Starfield
science fiction by Scottish writers

Edited by
Duncan Lunan

A loving re-creation of a classic collection of Scottish science fiction.

Published by Shoreline of Infinity

Publications
paperback, 240pp £11.95
ISBN 978-1-9997002-2-5

Stories and poems by

Angus MacVicar

Chris Boyce

David John Lee

Naomi Mitchison

Janice Galloway

Louise Turner

Angus McAllister

Edwin Morgan

Elsie Donald

William King

David Crooks

alburt plethora

Richard Hammersley

Alasdair Gray

Donald Malcolm

Duncan Lunan

Archie Roy

Cover: Sydney Jordan

www.shorelineofinfinity.com

The Walls of Tithonium Chasma

Tim Major

Halliday pauses at the window that curves around the loading bay of Tharsis Foxglove. His bare arms reflect the pale red of the sky. The nicks and cuts on the window, the result of dust storms, are a complex net.

Are the sculptors really still out there? He imagines the three of them, free of the suffocating atmosphere of the base. Working, or just patrolling the surface aimlessly. It would be difficult to blame them if they never returned.

He continues along the curved passageway, moving away from the living quarters and the rest of the team. It seems unreasonable, stashing the aye-ayes out here beside the trucks and rovers in the workshop. He traces a finger along the lockers, counting up. Ai403, Ai404, Ai405 absent serving in the chapel, Ai406. Should they have given them names? People had, with the early models, back home. But they had been companions rather than tools.

The moulded faces gaze back at him from within shrouds of dustproof sheeting. Naked as the day they were born. At the touch of a panel, Ai407 slides out, suspended by the armpits on two extending rods. Some way to sleep.

What's the hold-up? The boot process gets slower each time. The aye-aye's smooth mask twitches. The corners of each empty eyepit flicker with fine motor calibrations. It feels intrusive, watching an aye-aye wake. Halliday keeps still to allow its recognition software to kick in.

"Bring a trundler to the doors," he says, "I'll meet you there."

Ai407 moves away, its smooth feet padding softly on the shop floor.

Once he has suited up, Halliday slides himself into the passenger seat of the trundler. Ai407 does not turn to watch him as he struggles to arrange his legs into a comfortable position.

"Let's go."

The aye-aye raises both of its handless arms. Each stubby end glows blue as it interfaces with the onboard navigation system. The hatch door of the workshop rises silently and then they are outside.

Copper-coloured storm clouds have gathered in the distance, beyond the Valles Marineris. Other members of the team have talked about seeing clouds like these in dreams. They say that their dreams are more vivid, these days. Halliday himself doesn't dream, or doesn't remember.

He turns to look at the closed bay. The hatch is invisible from outside, fitted flush to the curve of the building. Behind the loading bay the spokes and bubbles of the living quarters emerge only slightly from their protective hills of dust. The buildings are sculpted from the same dull red as the Martian rock beneath.

"There's no chance the storm will head this way?" he says.

"There is a chance," the aye-aye replies.

"Quantify."

"Six per cent."

They travel in silence until they reach the end of the dirt track from the base. Halliday realises that he has always thought of it as a winding driveway, as if the base is a country house on Earth. They should sculpt a row of trees to line the edges of the road, do the job properly. The trundler slows to a halt.

"Where is our destination?" the aye-aye says.

"I don't know yet." Halliday fishes the screen from the pocket of his suit and unrolls it on his lap. It displays a map, preprogrammed by Aitchison in logistics. The base is marked in green and their own position is a throbbing orange dart. At a point five times the distance they have travelled hangs a parallelogram outlined in black. Its edges shift constantly. "Somewhere between F4 and F7, west of Tharsis Fuchsia. Get close and we'll take it from there."

The ground is rougher here. Halliday lurches to one side, pushing against Ai407's slick shoulder to right himself.

"You're not from the chapel, right?" he says.

"No. Ai406 and below service the chapel."

Halliday nods. A decade ago most colonists would have been horrified at the thought of religion thriving on Mars. When the Foxglove council had displayed the blueprints for the chapel sculpture, the reaction back home had been one of polite disgust.

He looks outside as they push through the first of the half-pipes that lead to the plains. Its sculpted walls are perfectly smooth. Only the upper edges are frayed, where the regolith has been scooped and shifted by the wind.

He glances at the moving shape on the screen. "Hey, aren't you all on the same network? All of you aye-ayes, and the sculptors?"

"Yes, we share bandwidth."

"Aitchison says there are three missing. They left last week to begin sculpting the new storehouse, west of here. Can you hear them?" He slides a finger along one of the blades at the edge of the map to reveal Aitchison's brief. "They're models SC33 to 35."

Ai407 turns its head as if straining to listen. "They're out on the periphery. I can barely feel them."

"They've been out there for days. What are they doing?"

Ai407's smooth lips move before speaking, as if rehearsing a response. "Sculpting."

Once they have crossed the sculpted bridge that connects Foxglove to the other regions, they emerge onto the plains proper. The sunlight, though filtered through the cloud of red dust and the tinted windscreen, stings Halliday's eyes. He feels a sense of freedom at seeing the bare rocks that litter the desert to either side. They are unsculpted, unchanged, unchanging. Tharsis Foxglove will never extend this far and yet they are still close enough that no new base will be constructed here either. This space will remain preserved, an area of natural beauty, or perhaps natural ugliness.

The trundler finds a smooth route. The jolting lessens.

"Stop here." Halliday pushes his way out of the vehicle and kneels, one gloved palm on the ground. The regolith is hard and compacted. It must have been pressed flat by the sculptors.

43

Back in the passenger seat he says, "Keep to the same route they took. Should prevent us from hitting any dead ends."

They reach a rise. From here Halliday can see the smoothed route winding west around the boulders. It is less direct than seems optimum. He remembers Sunday outings on his father's motorbike, to Ullswater and beyond. His father would say, "Never take the direct road when there's a scenic route in the offing".

The trundler gathers speed as it sweeps downhill. The parallelogram on the screen shrinks.

"We're closing in on their location." Halliday watches as the shape dwindles to a point. Soon, it is replaced by three faint blue specks in a cluster.

"Hey, stop. We've overshot them somehow." He looks out of the rear window. The desert is vast and light. None of the boulders are large enough to hide a sculptor.

He jabs at blades onscreen, pulling up the brief and then the nav calibration. He swings open the door and clambers up onto the roof of the vehicle. From here he can see that the terrain ahead is not as blank as the desert behind them. A dark ripple crosses the horizon. A canyon. The sculptors must be somewhere below them.

"How close are we to Ius Chasma?" he says.

"The nearest tributary canyon is one kilometre from here, directly ahead."

"Keep driving. Follow the road." Halliday has never ventured as far as the Valles Marineris, despite the proximity of Foxglove to some of the canyons. He looks down. Without being conscious of it, he has buckled his restraining seatbelt.

At the mouth of Ius Chasma the smoothed route takes a dogleg turn. The trundler stops at the summit and Halliday stares into the depths of the canyon. The rock walls are more orange than red.

"The road continues downwards," the aye-aye says.

"Take it," Halliday says.

The descent is giddying. The sculptors have only flattened an area wide enough to allow themselves to return without obstacle. The right caterpillar tread of the trundler runs on rougher ground, close enough to the edge to make Halliday grit his teeth.

"They're scheduled to be way east of here," he says, trying to distract himself. "Equidistant between Foxglove and Fuchsia, that was the council brief for the storehouse. And they haven't even started building. What the hell are they doing down here?"

The aye-aye pauses before answering. "Sculpting."

They reach the floor of Ius Chasma. Halliday wipes his forehead with the arm of his suit. The trundler lurches from side to side. The smooth road now winds in tighter turns than before.

"Forget the road," Halliday says, "Just follow its general direction."

The right wall of the canyon is a steep hill of rubble. It must be the result of landslides. Sunlight plays on the wall to the left of the trundler but the floor is in shade. Halliday glances down at the screen. The three dots are to the east, close. He sees the Foxglove bridge arc above. They have backtracked to arrive beneath their earlier route. These canyons criss-cross more than he realised.

"We are entering Tithonium Chasma," the aye-aye says.

Until now the walls have appeared fractured and rough. Here, their surfaces look as smooth as the sculpted road. A light swirl of ash dances ahead of them. Red-hued light blooms from a semi-circular passage.

Ai407 turns its blank face towards Halliday.

"What's that look for?" he says. "Carry on, that way." He points ahead, then pulls his hands under his thighs. He feels suddenly conscious of the aye-aye's own stubby limbs.

Red light bathes the trundler as they enter the passage. Before Halliday's eyes have adjusted to the light he hears a noise that is tinnier than the hum of the motor. It sounds like a mouse scratching below floorboards.

The walls of Tithonium Chasma are pillar-box red. The canyon is enormous, as if this is the true Martian surface and everything above is mountainous.

He sees the squat, tractor-like sculptors immediately, even though they are dwarfed by the rockface. One of them scratches at the right wall of the canyon. A cloud of dust rises around its suction funnel. The other two are facing away from the trundler as if surveying the work of their colleague.

Halliday peers up at the walls. Breath fogs the inside of his helmet, clearing from the top down. First he sees a sculpted stone bicycle that leans against a boulder. Further along the canyon, stepping stones dot a stream with static, sculpted wave crests. A young boy is frozen mid-leap with just the tip of one shoe touching rounded stone.

He cranes his neck. Standing apart from the canyon wall is a structure that towers above him, somehow too large for him to have noticed straight away. It is a steep hill with more stone waves lapping at its base. On top of the hill is a sculpted building with sheer sides that reflect the red light. Its towers are almost the height of the canyon walls.

He senses Ai407 standing beside him. The aye-aye is staring upwards at the wall where the sculptor is still at work. Here, the rock has been carved into less representative forms. It takes Halliday several seconds before he sees that it is the enormous figure of a man. His body is distorted, bent forward into a loping run. Flames surround his head like a lion's mane. His mouth is wide open and twisted in agony.

"Jesus," Halliday says. His voice is little more than a breath, "What is this?"

He flinches as Ai407 says, "It is a nightmare."

"But who the hell has nightmares like that?"

The aye-aye shields its eyes.

"I do."

✻

Halliday forces a smile as Reverend Corstorphine steeples his fingers and settles into his chair, which is the only fully complete item of furniture in the chapel. Though the structure of the building was completed a month ago, backlogs at the Sandcastle sculpting foundry have delayed the pews. Only a hanging tapestry smuggled from Earth interrupts the bare white walls. It is embroidered with the words, 'The sky above proclaims his handiwork'.

"I have long suspected as much," Corstorphine says. The chair creaks.

"That they have nightmares?" Halliday says.

46

Corstorphine chuckles. "Your sons and your daughters shall prophesy, and your young men shall see visions, and your old men shall dream dreams."

Halliday wishes that there were a desk to separate them. "Except the aye-ayes aren't sons and daughters, or men, young or old."

In the opposite corner of the chapel, beside a tea tray on the floor, a kettle comes to the boil. Corstorphine crosses the room and bends to fill two mugs, handing one to Halliday. "It's only instant, I'm afraid."

Halliday accepts the mug and wishes he hadn't. He would prefer to take nothing from Corstorphine. People like him charge interest on a debt, however small. Before he knows it, he'll be given chapel duties like the rest of the team. He had been rash to approach the Reverend with his findings. It had been a moment of weakness.

Corstorphine sips his drink noisily, then rests the mug on his belly. "Dreams are only echoes. Expressions of an experience not fully processed. The dreams are not the thing. Tell me again what you saw."

Halliday describes the scene at Tithonium Chasma again. It is easy, as he has thought of it often in the days that have passed. The boy in the stream, the castle, the burning man. What can it mean?

When he finishes, he rubs his face. He has drunk the coffee without realising it. "It's a vision of Earth, that much is clear. And, as far as I know, Foxglove's aye-ayes were constructed back there, then shipped over with the rest of us. But that doesn't really explain anything. What do you make of it all?"

"Well. I'm happy to say that it supports a pet theory of mine," Corstorphine says. "I must thank you for coming to me with this information."

Smug bastard. Halliday resents the bait but takes it anyway. "What's your theory?"

The Reverend's eyes travel upwards. Above him is only a prismatic white space.

"That the aye-ayes possess souls."

✳

47

After Halliday awakens it, Ai407 stands loose-limbed in the centre of the workshop. Sleepy and sulky. It waits for him to speak.

"Who is your father?" Halliday says, finally.

Ai407 doesn't answer.

Maybe he phrased the question badly. He bends to look into Ai407's sunken eyepits. "Who is your AI template?"

The aye-aye replies instantly. "Felix Ransome, the son of Professor Elias Ransome."

Halliday gasps. "*The* Elias Ransome?"

"Professor Elias Ransome."

So these aye-ayes were among the first on Mars, or at least their AI subroutines were. All this time, Halliday has been working alongside antiques.

Back on Earth, twenty years ago, Elias Ransome had been a key player in aye-aye technology. He worked for years, developing faster and more efficient chips and behaviour routines. But the true breakthrough wasn't an issue of computing power. Ransome bestowed on the aye-ayes the gift of imagination.

Aye-ayes were technically advanced, but in practical terms they were imbeciles. Give a man a fish and you feed him for a day; teach a man to fish and you feed him for a lifetime. Teach an aye-aye to fish and it'd bring you shoals and shoals, fine. But give it a single fish without also providing clear instructions and it would just stare at the fish for a lifetime. What was missing was imagination, and Ransome provided it. Or rather, his then eight-year-old son, Felix, donated it via an imprint of his brain patterns.

Halliday waves to dismiss Ai407. The aye-aye clambers back onto its plinth and arranges its short arms so that its weight is supported by the extended rods. As the rods retract, carrying the aye-aye backwards into the housing, Ai407 turns its blank face towards Halliday. Halliday shudders. He glances at the rows of aye-ayes in their sarcophagus-like closets. They are all on the same network. They are family. They are all little Felix Ransome's children, able to function only because they had once been inspired by his gift for invention and his developing moral code.

Their blank faces seem less inert. Halliday sees the subtle flinches of sleep.

Reverend Corstorphine makes a show of being engrossed in his book. Halliday enjoys the idea that perhaps he is reading the Bible for the first time. All of the clergy here are amateurs. They are only appropriating religion in response to market demands.

"You don't believe it yourself," Halliday says.

Corstorphine glances down at the book, for a moment misunderstanding what Halliday is referring to. He removes his spectacles, which have pinched craters into the bridge of his nose.

"I wouldn't have returned," Halliday says, "But I can't let you go on like this. It's a farce." There are now only a handful of the team, including himself, who still do not attend Sunday services. From overheard conversations in the canteen it is clear that recent sermons have been filled with talk of the aye-aye's souls.

The Reverend's neat goatee is a dark smile beneath his lips. "I merely repeated what you yourself told me."

They stand side by side to look through the scarred window. The chapel is at the highest point of Tharsis Primrose. They can see over the sculpted barriers to the crescent-shaped sand dunes that shuffle slowly across the Martian plains.

"And the trips to Tithonium Chasma?" Halliday speaks slowly to prevent his voice from cracking. "You encouraged the fools to take those pilgrimages, too?"

"Your colleagues have simply found meaning in an astounding phenomenon. It is comforting to know that God speaks to the aye-ayes as well as to us."

Halliday's shoulders slacken. "I think I understand. You assert that God rules the aye-ayes. So then, if we ever do find life out there, we can assume that God's the boss of them too. Everyone and everything answers to Him. Right?"

He sees Corstorphine's raised eyebrow reflected in the window.

"It's blindness," Halliday continues. "You're showing God's work where there is none, only engineering. You're encouraging these people to ask the wrong questions and find the wrong answers, just to promote your faith." Annoyed at his own lack of restraint, he changes tack. "When did you leave Earth? Ninety-seven, eight?"

"Yes. Ninety-eight."

"And you're smart enough to have read the small print during sign-up. We all donated. Straightforward scanning and uploading of our brain patterns for potential use in templating." A hollow laugh. "I bet the idea appealed to you. Providing moral guidance to the aye-ayes."

Like Corstorphine, Halliday had been at school in the eighties, back when 'aye-aye' equated to merely 'vacuum cleaner' or 'cook'. Then there had been a miraculous leap in their capabilities at the end of the decade, due to the brain-pattern breakthrough. He remembers the TV shows. Aye-ayes on obstacles courses, aye-ayes flying planes. There was much talk about the march of technological progress. It was the stuff of dreams and school projects.

Halliday retrieves a screen from his jacket pocket and unrolls it on the lectern, ignoring Corstorphine's protests. He pulls up an image browser and, after a minute's search, turns the screen towards the Reverend. The screen shows a photo of a blunt, high-walled castle on top of a hillock that spirals upwards from the sea like a snail's shell. "There. That's the building I saw in Tithonium Chasma."

"I know it," Corstorphine says. He sounds fascinated, despite himself. "That's Lindisfarne Castle."

"It was," Halliday says. "It's just rubble now. Did you know that Elias Ransome died there during the war?" He shudders, remembering the news-report images of the firestorms after the bombs. Flames and flesh.

The Reverend's face shows recognition of the name. "And the boy in the stream?"

"Felix Ransome, of course. All those things were his memories, expressed by the aye-ayes through the sculptors. They all share bandwidth. Felix Ransome witnessed his father's death and then he relived it in his dreams. So the aye-ayes do too."

Streaks glisten on Reverend Corstorphine's cheeks. Embarrassed, Halliday busies himself rolling up the screen. "Tell me again that you believe the aye-ayes have souls."

Corstorphine runs his fingers along the edges of the lectern. His hands stop shaking. When he looks up again, his eyes are cold. "We all require mysteries. The colonists do."

"Not mysteries. Lies."

✳

In the days and weeks that follow, Halliday approaches nobody. Even once the enthusiasm for pilgrimages to Tithonium Chasma has diminished, the congregation accept the sculptures as proof of the all-encompassing purview of God. Halliday spends his free time alone in his cabin.

He does not only think of Felix Ransome. Halliday donated his own brain patterns twelve years ago, just like Felix, just like all the other would-be colonists. Aye-ayes inspired by his thoughts may still be in service, somewhere on Mars. And if they are, might they not dream his dreams, just like the Foxglove aye-ayes dreamt Felix's?

Except Halliday doesn't dream. This in itself makes the prospect more fascinating to him. What would his aye-ayes, if they exist, tell him about himself? He dredges his memories for moments that might hold up against Felix's firestorms. The early death of Yvonne, his sister. The late death of Constable, his dog.

He must know which of his memories defines him.

Time passes. He makes some calls.

✳

Four years later, a contact of a contact is finally able to help. Halliday is directed towards the remote outpost of Wigwam in the Iani Chaos region. His transfer request takes months to be processed and is met with incredulity by the authorities. While the Tharsis region is as bleak as anywhere on Mars, at least there are people there.

Not only does Iani Wigwam contain no human employees, the small base houses no humanoid aye-ayes either. In the workshop there are only rows of sculptors with their suction funnels neatly recessed into their blunt bodies. The single AI processing unit is a white, cuboid block that crouches in the centre of a tiny control room. It hums like a fridge. It has no auditory receptors and no input panel. Halliday stands before it and wonders whether this white box really does hold the blueprint of his brain pattern. Whether it thinks as he thinks. Whether it dreams his dreams.

His only function is to assess and repair the sculptors. It is the first such intervention in a decade and is barely needed; the sculptors are capable of performing many of the repair tasks themselves. He sleeps, reads novels, and maintains the sculptors and the exterior of the base. He waits.

After three weeks, without warning or ceremony, the processing unit sends a silent command to one of the sculptors. Halliday is asleep when it leaves through its low catflap door. Lacking a trundler, he pulls on his suit and follows on foot.

He wanders among the mesas and hillocks of Iani Chaos. Some of the flat-topped blocks are so tall and thin that they could be Earth skyscrapers.

While he walks he reviews the events of his life. He orders and ranks the images. He remembers the time he believed, for an hour or so, that one his girlfriends had shot herself. He remembers becoming lost in the forest near to his house and spending the night beneath the stars. He remembers another girlfriend and the loss of his virginity. He remembers his parents and his friends. He remembers deaths. Bodies piled upon bodies.

He heads away from the distant bump of Iani Wigwam. The terrain underfoot is hard rock so there is no evidence of the sculptor's tracks. He chooses directions at random. He is prepared to explore the area all day in the hope of finding the sculptor.

At a sandy junction between mesas, he sees traces of tyre tracks. They continue south and meander from side to side between the rock outcrops. They are wandering just like he is wandering, as if pre-empting his steps.

They are his. The steps, the AI fridge, the sculptors. Perhaps he and they identify so strongly that they can even predict where he will walk.

A bulky shape appears ahead. Halliday has to squint to see that it is not natural rock. As he approaches he recognises that it is a sculptor.

He groans. The sculptor is tilted to one side and its bulky chassis appears warped. Has it sunk into soft ground? No, beneath the dust layer the rock seems firm. The suction funnel is low to the ground. It had been in the process of hoovering up the regolith, ready for it to be reconstituted as sculpture.

But what was it sculpting before it became trapped? Did this sculptor dream his dreams?

He skirts around it, keeping it at arm's length in case of serious malfunction.

The rear panel of the sculptor hangs open at ninety degrees. It must have been mid-way through compressing and carving the regolith. Halliday bends to examine the object that lies on its side within the tray.

It is a tulip with cupped petals half-open.

He reaches out to touch it. The tulip is cold and hard. It means nothing to him. If he dreamt, he would not dream of tulips. He would dream of…

But the only images that occur to him are of aye-ayes and sculptors. Sculpting, dreaming. His obsession, for years now. His life.

He notices that there is something peculiar about the machine. On closer inspection the chassis appears totally off-kilter. It is a distorted caricature of its usual appearance.

Hesitantly, he places a hand on the chassis. Instead of metal he feels cold, pressed sand.

He begins to weep.

This is not a sculptor, but a sculpture.

Tim Major is the author of *Machineries of Mercy, You Don't Belong Here* and a book about the 1915 silent film, Les Vampires. In 2019 Titan Books will publish *Snakeskins* and Luna Press will publish his first collection, *And the House Lights Dim.* Tim's stories have appeared in *Best of British SF* and *The Best Horror of the Year.* www.cosycatastrophes.com

Goddess with a Human Heart

Jeannette Ng

The speaker outside my window splutters to life. Between the static and the distorted, mechanical voice it is impossible to make out the time being announced.

But I know. I have three hours left.

My hand creeps unconsciously to my chest and rests on my beating, fluttering heart. Caged in bones and bound in flesh, it longs for something more. It has a fate apart from me. It aches.

I turn on my bunk to face the window and its cramped view of the street outside. I can see the edge of the ziggurat from here. It is early and the lights are beginning to spark. It is pretty, in a way.

I remember the first time I saw the Goddess in the temple. My legs and feet had been sore from climbing the great ziggurat. I had huddled at the top of steps, frowning at my shiny child shoes, their heels stained with machine oil. My doll of knotted rags was tucked under my arm. I chewed my braid as people streamed past me. I heard my mother call.

I had looked up and all those petty, pretty things fell away.

The Goddess who Listens to the Suffering of the World.

She was arranged cross-legged among and upon the endless tangle of wires and tubes and pipes that fed Her. They are Her thousand hands and thousand eyes. Above Her, shrouded in a thick haze of machine smoke, were the thick coils of Her thinking, blinking databanks. In days of old, She was depicted with a spread of arms behind her back, like the spokes of a great wheel. Each arm would end in a hand with an eye at the palm. Each would hold something different: a sword, a book, a fan, a branch, a reminder of all she could do. But now, we know Her true form.

I felt Her eyes on me and was suddenly aware of my own inconsequence as a child: all plump cheeks, stubby limbs and cute sharpened teeth.

I looked for Her face; it was under a crown of spiralling glass cables that feathered the light into a dizzying array of colour, obscuring most of her features. I could just about make out half-closed, sunken eyes and high, sharp cheekbones and the shadow of lips. Her cheeks were stained red with machine oil from her crown of cables. I imagined she looked upon us with infinite, ineffable wisdom.

Her real, mortal arms had long been severed and had been arranged like the petals of a lotus around Her torso. One of her hands held a tiny light that cast a red glow onto the papery, preserved skin of her arms. Her robes seemed to whisper gently with Her every breath. One of the folds had shifted from Her shoulder and I could see the rows of glinting medical staples down her left breast.

Three hours. Or rather, a little less now.

I am older now, but part of me will always remain that awe-struck little girl. It is that little girl's heart that the Goddess needs in Her. The priests have counted the days and it is time. We owe it to Her. And we need Her.

I curl into myself. The priests will be here for me soon. My eyes fall on the pale green robe that hangs in wait for me. I shudder; clutch the sheets closer to myself. My stomach clenches and the urge to hurl pulses at the back of my throat. I try to breathe.

Again and again, my mind returns to the stories of the past, of how the gods and goddesses walked among us. Always at the end of the tale, the deities would cast off the mortal skins they wore and reveal themselves to their followers.

Ages rise and fall. Each age begins with blood and ends with blood, for that is how the days are measured. The people are transformed and a new sun rises from the ashes.

The bright sun of the fifth age, Left-Handed Hummingbird, was slain by his sister the moon, She whose Face is Painted with Bells. She led the stars in a war against him and we nourished our sun with sacrifices of blood and bone. We called ourselves the People of the Sun. For a while, it seemed enough.

Until, of course, one day, when it wasn't. Our brave, proud warrior sun was poisoned by his treacherous sister. It darkened and cooled and we gave up more and more of ourselves to feed him. The war of the heavens continued, and as Left-Handed Hummingbird dimmed, we knew it was the end of the fifth age and we knew our deaths to be written. It is the way of the world, that each age end in blood and fire.

That was when the Goddess appeared.

From beyond the darkness, She found us. She heard our suffering. She was the reflection that hid in the obsidian mirror of our pantheon. She snaked from its ink-black surface like smoke and promised us life. She saved us from the darkness and became our new sun.

We built our new world around Her, though we gave it an old name: Aztlán. Enthroned in Her temple atop the greatest ziggurat ever built by mortal hands, She sits at the heart of our metropolis. She hears our suffering, shapes our world and illuminates our darkness. Her databanks arrange and organise every aspect of our great metropolis, from the times of the cloudrail to every suncoil that shines on every waterfield.

I swallow, though my mouth is still dry and my stomach unsettled. I try not to think of all the things I will leave unfinished in my room. Scrap-rag serials I will never know the endings of. That scrap of knitting I will never finish. The milk that will expire after I breathe my last. I should be finishing things, not turning over and over in my bunk. I want to pace, but there isn't the space in my cramped room.

The heart that beats in me is not my own. It belongs to the Goddess and it has always belonged to Her. I am not a sacrifice; I am merely a vessel for Her heart, a mortal skin that She needs to shed.

I imagine the obsidian scalpel against my breast, and my stomach knots. This mortal skin has felt too much already. We are meant to surrender Her heart to Her when it is still unburdened by such feelings.

Perhaps I am already too old for this.

It has been said that as the days are counted, the human heart within the Goddess hardens to the sounds of our suffering. With each beat, it turns Her away from us. Humans, after all, are not made for boundless mercy. We are small, petty creatures, finite in our loves and likes.

And so she needs a new heart every three years. Before they break.

In the last count of days and years, heretics have disrupted the transplanting of the Goddess' heart. The blessed hour passed and the black scalpel did not fall. Last time, I sat in this room wide-eyed and full of hope. I remember sitting on the edge of my bed, feet dangling impatiently as I waited for Father Itztli. I was fearless, then, and I knew only love. I wanted only to surrender to the Goddess what was Hers by right.

It has since been three long years.

With shaking hands, I undress. I resist the urge to study the dark, gangly shape in my mirror as I reach for the robe. Vanity will do me no good now. The synthetic is crisp against my skin. The back ties are awkward, but I manage. There is no need to be neat. I bind my old running shoes to my feet. I try not to think of how this will be the last time I wear them.

The yellow streetlights flicker and I glance out. Hunched figures in white and red shuffle down the street. I watch the steel door slide open and the three shapes disappear through. I can smell the pungent mix of incense and machine oil before I can hear their footsteps.

They are here.

The door gives a beep before it opens. Father Itztli steps in, followed by two other priests. They smile at me, bowing their heads gravely and gesturing me peace.

"Are you ready, little one?" says Itztli. He is beautiful, as all priests are. His hair falls in a mass of turquoise and garnet augments.

I bite my tongue. Desire coils and uncoils around the heart that isn't mine. Irrationally, I want to hear my name from his lips, but I know he cannot bring himself to say it.

"Are you ready?" he repeats.

"As ready as the sun is to set at dusk." My voice sounds hollow and the ritualised words devoid of meaning. I remember the hours I have spent meditating upon them, for they would be my last. It is strange to speak of these things in terms of ancient celestial phenomena. "Thank you, Itztli."

For a moment, he hesitates. He licks his lips and very slowly, he swallows. "Give us a moment."

"But –" says one of the priests.

"We are five minutes ahead. It will be fine."

The two priests exchange unreadable looks and leave us. As the door glides shut behind them, I find myself shaking. I am breathing heavily.

"Yoltzin," he begins, but I throw myself at him, winding my arms tightly around him. His breath catches. My fingers tangle into his robes and the heart that isn't mine aches.

I know this heart loves him because he is Her high priest. And I know I love him for shallow reasons: because he has dark eyes, because his hair is beautiful, because his voice is soft and enchanting. It changes nothing.

We stay like this for long moments, him rigid and still in my arms, me clutching desperately at him. The knotted cord of his body tightens under my touch. He has balled his hands into fists. He dares not touch me.

But he breathes my name again and I am gasping, choking on dry sobs. I press my face against his stiff linen tunic. The strings of turquoise around his neck dig into me.

I feel as though I am drowning. I remember the polluted waters of the Culiacán engulfing me as I plunged into them. It was Itztli, still an acolyte then, who was drowning and I rescued him. I dragged him from the dark waters of the canal. As he choked water from his lungs, he uttered Her divine name. Over and over in his delirium, he called out to Her. I did not know what to do, but I studied the sharp angles of his face and stroked the damp curls of his hair. I wanted to press my lips to his and kiss the name of the Goddess on them. I imagined it to be a sacrament; I understood so very little of the flesh.

My rescue of him was how they recognised me as the Goddess' vessel. I cling to him now as he did to me then.

The door beeps. I step from him and try to compose myself. The door opens.

They drape a heavy jacket over my shoulders and we leave. The streets are cold at this hour and the drains are steaming. The sky is a sickly yellow. A haze clings to the city like dust on windows. Aztlán is beginning to stir. The sight of people fumbling with their keys, walking from their homes, waiting for the skyrail all remind me how selfish I have been in my thoughts of Itztli.

The speakers choke out incoherent sounds. Two hours.

I have lived for long enough. Far longer than most vessels. I have had a room of my own, an unimaginable luxury. I shared one with siblings for most of my childhood. We used to fight each other for the crackling, foil-lined blankets, tumbling over and over in the dark.

We wind our way through the bleakness and into the ziggurat. Itztli casts a glance behind but his eyes do not settle on me. The steel doors close behind us. The air is suddenly heavier and warmer. It presses damp against my skin. I feel a low hum in my bones.

I shed my shoes and the jacket; acolytes take them from me. I briefly wonder if they will clothe another of the Goddess' vessels. The metal floor is warm against my bare feet. I am led to a steel operating table. For a moment, everything feels too still. I want to bolt, but I think again of the Goddess, of the city's peopled streets, of Itztli, and I calm myself. I lie down, stiffly.

A priest in a turquoise mask approaches. A shock of glass cables and feathers frame the fragmented shapes of the mosaic face. I know it to be Itztli. With gloved hands, Itztli presses the laryngeal mask to my face. I breathe deeply from it.

Before the blackness claims me, I see Itztli dip his head to kiss the mask.

\#

Light.

Warm, brilliant light washes over me in waves. I am in endless fields of light, each arcing beam a stalk, refracting into rainbows. I find myself wandering through the light, hands flitting through its feathery fronds. An indistinct lullaby from my childhood threads its way through the breeze.

The Goddess is crying.

She is a small child, curled like a sea-slug shell in a sobbing heap. Her hair sprawls out in a web, all sharp angles like the etchings on a circuit board, or the lines on a map of the thirteen heavens. She looks up at me with eyes that seem to have seen all of time. She reaches out to me with a thousand hands. She is looking at me and through me.

It suddenly seems so foolish to think that a change of mortal hearts every few years can fool a Goddess who Listens to the Suffering of the World. Tears stream from her face like light, like music, like waves. She hears every sorrow and feels the pain of this imperfect, created world. She cries because she cannot save us all.

I am wearing a garland of red flowers. I take it bleeding from my neck and drape it around hers. The Goddess smiles and closes Her eyes. The flowers bleed and bleed. Dark bruises blossom under her skin.

She crumples, still smiling with mottled skin, lying in a pool of infinite red.

✳

My eyes open.

I did not expect that. There is an aching, empty numbness across my chest. I try to sit up, but I seem to have no control over my limbs. A draught ghosts over my skin and I shiver. Bright colours dance at the edge of my vision.

"Don't move." It is Itztli's voice, gentle and firm. My head cannot turn to see him. "I'll prop you up."

My hand flies to my chest, or rather, tries to. My shoulder twitches and my left arm flails. Half my chest feels numb, though I can make out something heavily thudding inside me. Thoughts stumble and stagger in my clouded brain.

"What... my heart... the Goddess..."

He laughs, a sound I never thought to hear again. "Your heart of flesh and blood is in Her. Whatever good that does Her now." As he moves into view, I see him as though for the first time. His hair has been crudely shorn close to the scalp; he looks different without the shock of beads and wire augments. His shadowed eyes seem smaller without the dark lines. I notice again the sharp angles of his face, the sharp arch of his brow, the length of his lashes. The numbness in my chest deepens.

"She needs a heart," I murmur. I do not know if he can hear me.

Itztli arranges me into a sitting position. He is gentle, but it matters not. I can barely feel his touch. We are in a narrow corridor, dark but for a flicking light some paces ahead. Cables and pipes run the length of the walls and there is a low, persistent humming. There are numbers and markings, but they mean nothing to me.

"Why, when Her mind is stored in coiled databanks, does She need a human heart?" asks Itzli. "Why when they can make Her blinking wire-framed eyes and pulsing plastic innards can they not make Her a heart? It is nonsensical."

"But it is Her heart." The colours at the edge of my vision threatened to overwhelm me, flitting brilliance across my eyes.

He shakes his head. "That doesn't matter now. She won't survive it. I've..." There is an alien note of bitterness in his voice. "Don't you want to know how I saved you?"

"I'm supposed to be..." I grit my teeth; I do not want to use the word.

"I've put a part of Her in you." He glances down the corridor. "It's not exactly Her heart, but there really isn't much more to a heart than a series of valves and pumps. So it wasn't hard to adapt. There was so much blood. I was scared... After I took out yours –"

"It is not mine. It is Hers," I insist, though my voice sounds hollow, like an echo. It is strange to think that there is a part of the divine machine inside me. He says nothing and the silence is heavy between us. Though my mouth is dry, I swallow. "Why did..."

I try to pull myself to my feet, but cannot.

"You'll need to be carried," he says and folds me into his arms. I do not protest. I lean heavily against him. He smells of disinfectant, blood and beeswax. "Neither of us can go back. Because of what..."

He does not finish the thought; he can no more speak of it than I can.

"I don't... I... why?" I force breath into my restricted lungs. "Why did you do that?"

"You saved me. That matters."

"The Goddess saved you."

"No." His voice is a whisper, but firm. I can feel him swallow. "She damned me. And you. It doesn't matter now. It is all sophistry."

"Of course it matters. It's the Goddess. She sees everything."

He gives a brief, bitter scoff of a laugh.

"She does. She listens to our suffering. She knows you. Her heart loved you because She saw your suffering. She understands." The pain that was vague and distant before is beginning to coalesce into a heavy, thudding knot in my chest. "She knows you did whatever you did. She knows we are down here. She allows it."

Pain devours up the numbness inside me; the shock is almost electric. I choke out a cry.

"The anaesthetics are probably... don't move. Just don't move." He swallows, trying to calm himself. "It'll be fine. It'll be fine." He slurs the words as though they were a litany. Fleetingly, he seems again that priest who taught me how to read, how to pray and how to drag a rope of thorns through my tongue.

My eyes flutter shut, but through the angry, mechanical rhythm of the thing inside me, I hear the clink of glass and metal. I hear the needle and syringe rather than feel it. Raw, wild colours roar through my vision before subsiding again into the black behind my eyelids.

When I reopen my eyes, the shapes in the dark seem sharper and cold, more keen.

"She hears us. Every day." I mouth to Itztli. "If She allowed this. Then this is. This is Her plan."

He closes his eyes. His face contorts; more emotion than I have ever seen him show in our years together. "We should keep moving."

I say nothing and he carries me down the corridors. I imagine we are in the disused underbelly of the ziggurat, but I do not do so with certainty. Itztli picks his way through increasingly twisted passages.

The outside is nothing more than shadows and shapes at the edge of my blurring vision. Itztli presses me close to his chest. I can hear his heart beat against me now. It is a closeness that I had previously hungered for.

The street corner speakers declare the hour. I guess it to be late given the colour of the lights. Judging from the quality of the speakers, we are in a rough quadrant of the city. I allow my eyes to drift shut and the pain to claim me. If I think only of the pain, concentrate on its myriad shades stretching and clenching inside me, I can keep from crying out. It hurts more when he sprints, but thankfully he does not do that often.

Itztli pauses several times before continuing. Each time, I hear his voice through the haze: "It'll be fine. It'll be fine."

Leaning on an archaic door to open it, we enter into a building. Voices greet him. Frantic, heartfelt concern melts into indistinct congratulations and curiosity.

"Is that it? That why you joined us?"

"I thought she'd be –"

"It's not as though the Goddess Herself is a looker."

That got a laugh from the others, though I can feel Itztli's grip on me tighten at the blasphemy. He sits but he does not put me down. I feel a wall against my back, but his arms are still around me.

The voices around us plan and plot. I follow more the cadence of the voices than the substance of their plans. There will be a new world and a new age, one without light and without a sun, watched over by no God.

✳

Days pass. I am bundled in the corner of the room, half-forgotten by most of the heretics. Itztli has been playing surgeon for them and he tends to me. I remember little but for a certain warmth of arms, a constant constricting pain and thin soup against my lips. I remember choking on blood and vomit. I remember needles and colours too bright to be real.

I also remember this:

"Are you awake?" Itztli whispers against my ear. I am still. I try to speak, but my throat contracts. The beat of the thing inside my chest feels odd and alien.

Distantly, I can feel fingertips following the angles of my face, stroking my hair, the line of my lips. "I'm sorry. I'm sorry I never told you, Yoltzin. But until I did what needed to be done, we could not speak the plan aloud. I know you believed. But She... The count of days is wrong. We are not the sixth age. We are but the death throes of the fifth. We are part of the catastrophe of the age's end. We are not living in a new and glorious age, we are merely the last of a dying one, needlessly dragging out the pain of our people. I am just ending what needs to be ended. I am just saving you."

Every word of his is heresy. I try to force open my eyes, but I do not have the strength. I breathe in shallow, swift gasps. I manage a low whimper of pain, but not words. The journey has been more taxing than either of us anticipated.

"The others will build a new world without the need for endless sacrifice. There will be no part in it for a priest old before his time, a priest with this much blood on his hands. There will be no part in it for an old sacrifice either, an old sacrifice who still believes. But I had to. I had to save you. I just...

"I killed the Goddess. I won't be able to tell you when you wake, but I need to say this now. I killed Her. I slipped a knife into Her heart when I stapled shut Her chest. She will bleed."

At the mention of blood, my mind turns to the red flowers and the blossoming bruises on the Goddess. In more ancient times, they called such human sacrifice a flowery death. It was said to be the most noble way to die. I remember the pictures we were shown as children, the men and women sprawled out in bright blossoms of blood, each splatter uncurling like a petal from their heart.

"She will bleed under Her skin," whispers Itztli. "The blood will clog the parts that are inside Her. She will lose too much. She will die before they notice."

"She…" The immensity of the realisation pushes me to form words. I croak them out despite the pain. "She wanted you to…"

Itztli recoils.

"She wanted you to. I saw Her. She showed me." I keep my eyes closed, but I fumble a hand towards Itztli. I stroke a finger down his jaw. His skin is cold, too cold. Instead of the suncoils and the skyrail, my mind returns to the smile I saw in my dream of light. It dawns on me, colours unravelling endlessly in my mind like all the sunrises I have only ever imagined, pressing grubby fingers on yellowing picbook pages. "She hears everything. She hears everyone. Even those who fight against her priests and her enforcers. She can only bear our sorrows and suffering for so long. She wanted you to end it. She wanted a new age."

"No." His voice is thick and warm against my ear. "This is not yours to forgive."

"There is nothing to forgive."

He does not believe me, but he holds me tighter, probably too tight. It barely matters through the drugs and the pain.

I try to focus on the way he and I fit together: my head on his shoulder, the tangle of his hands, the twining hold of his legs. I want to think only on the way his cold skin and the knot of his scars feel against me. I want desperately for this to be the only thing that matters. He has torn out most of his augments and he smells of old blood and sweat. I wonder if he sought to flay off his skin this way, in a penance of sorts. He does not carry his crime lightly.

Pain cuts through these thoughts and the erratic beat of the mechanical heart consumes me; I hear it echo in my ears.

I cannot forget.

❈

Look above, child.

The sun you see today is not the sun that shone above the first people. Five ages and five tyrant suns have risen and fallen. Ours will one day fall as well.

The first was the Lord of Near and Nigh. But his brother, the Feathered Serpent, was envious of how the once crippled god

66

shone, so he knocked him from the firmament with a stone club. Without the sun, the people were lost to darkness and in that darkness they turned on one another. They consumed each other and in their barbarism, they became jaguars.

The next age was ruled by the Feathered Serpent. He died in wind and rage, with its people clinging to trees and becoming monkeys.

He Who Is Made of Earth ascended as the next sun but his wife was kidnapped and thus he wallowed in narcissistic grief. Besieged by prayers, he destroyed the world in a rain of fire. To escape, the people became birds, soaring above the flaming sea.

The fourth age ended with its people becoming fish as the goddess had a heart too soft, too kind and too broken. She flooded the world with her black tears. A man and woman survived, hiding in a hollow tree, but found themselves being turned into dogs by the gods. We do not live in a time of just gods.

The fifth sun, Left-Handed Hummingbird, demanded unending sacrifice of hearts upon his altars of blood and bone. But the moon, She whose Face is Painted with Bells, knew this to be unjust, so she made war upon him night after night. But war was a stalemate and unable to witness the suffering of the people, she poisoned her own brother.

Then came the time of blood and burning. We have lived in the shadow of the fifth age, in its final breaths. As with the end of every age, the trials made us into beasts as we cling to survival. The Goddess with the Human Heart could not bear the suffering any longer and the Last Priest killed her in an act of mercy, ending the time of sacrifice.

And so dawned a sixth age. There is a new sun and a new people, but tyrants do not live forever. I hear the Last Priest and the Girl with the Divine Heart wander the wastes. I hear they are near.

The wheel of the heavens will turn again.

Jeannette Ng was born in Hong Kong and now lives in Durham. She designs and plays live roleplaying games, makes costumes and writes speculative fiction. She was presented with the 2018 Newcomer Award by the British Fantasy Society for her debut novel *Under The Pendulum Sun* published by Angry Robot,

The Pink Life (La Vie En Rose)

Nathan Susnik

On Monday a crisply painted fire hydrant moved into the alcove next to my apartment building. On Tuesday it sang *La Boheme*. On Wednesday, *Carmen*. Today, *Der Vogelfänger*. The fire hydrant has digitally perfect tone and tenor. I walk past it twice a day on my way to work:

#operasingingfirehydrant #pureperfection

I reach my 85th floor office, greet my secretary, and look out at the architecture. The city is an art deco wonderland. #newyork1950s. Market reports waterfall down the Chrysler Building, splashing onto the Theatre des Champs-Elysees. A personal message blinks on the Empire State Building:

@rickstock538 – InComp/Filefunk merger approved. Buy!

I'm halfway through a reply when – flash – #newyork1950s is gone. An endless field of homogeneous, concrete skyscrapers in its place.

Flash – #newyork1950s.

Flash – endless concrete skyscrapers.

Flash – #newyork1950s.

Flash. Flash. Flash.

"Ava," I say.

"Yes Ms. van Kamp?" She comes in the room looking different from before, less than perfect. There's a pimple on her forehead, a large white head pressing out from a glowing red base.

Flash – Silky smooth.

Flash – Krakatoa.

"What do you see outside?" I say. She ambles to window, limping slightly. She shrugs.

"Buildings?"

"Nothing unusual?"

"Nothing," she says.

"Thank you, Ava. You can go." I sigh.

#whyisitalwaysme?

When she leaves, I message Dsense corp. Five seconds later (poof) they project a representative over the intercerebral computer.

"It's not an error with the iPerceive app. It must be a problem with your operating system ma'am," she says. "Turn iPerceive off."

"You can do that?"

"Do what?"

"Turn iPerceive off," I say. She winks.

"You'd be surprised how many people don't know that. But then again why in God's name would you want to turn it off? Anyway, if you have it on while it's glitching, it can be dangerous."

"Dangerous?"

"Yes, just between you and me, a client jumped in Niagara Falls last year thinking the water was cotton candy. Anyway, have the InComp run an update tonight while you sleep. That should solve the problem."

"I'm not paying for services this month," I say. She is as sweet as strawberries.

"Here at Dsense corp customer satisfaction is key. You won't be charged for services for the next two months. Plus we'll..." She pauses, scanning through her records, trying to find an app or addon that I don't have. "...we'll unlock AllGourmet level 5 for two months."

"Fine," I say.

I stare out the window. The shadows of concrete monstrosities darken the streets below. It's depressing, like being smothered with a soiled pillow.

"Serotonin levels decreasing. Go ahead and take the day off," advises LifeCoach app. It's good advice, and I should follow it. Since subscribing to LifeCoach my self-satisfaction levels have increased 523%, according to LifeCoach app. A message blinks from the dark streets:

@rickstock538: U buy?

I exhale, and LifeCoach tells me about the dangers of critically low neurotransmitters.

@laurenvankamp923: Technical problems, Plz take account till 2morrow! #vacationday

※

I board a transporter. Without iPerceive, darkness fills streets where sunlight formerly shone. There are considerably fewer flowers than usual, considerably fewer birds too, in fact no birds and no flowers; it's all trash and beggars, concrete and darkness.

I get home, and in the place of the #operasingingfirehydrant is a beggar. He's young, the left half of his face is scar tissue, his eyes are sunken, and his cheek bones are too sharp. Instead of singing opera, he's begging. He wants food. A wave of crumminess sweeps over me. LifeCoach calmly informs me about dangerous levels of something or other. I flip iPerceive back on.

Flash – *The Barber of Seville*.

Flash – homeless beggar.

Flash – Count Almaviva.

Flash – beggar.

iDentify kicks in:

*Ping – *Sergeant Steven Johnson, 32, earned a Silver Star and a Purple Heart in the second battle of Pyongyang...*

I interrupt the facial recognition app. Wait, a *second* battle of Pyongyang? When did that happen?

*Ping – *The Second battle of Pyongyang began on April...*

I interrupt WikiSearch app. On second thought, I really don't need to know.

Sergeant Johnson looks at me. He cocks his head like some kind of intelligent bird. It's clicked. He knows that I see him.

"Please," he says reaching out. I walk past. He follows. "I'm hungry," he says. I keep walking. He reaches to touch my shoulder. I jump away and he screams, grabbing his head. I exhale. At least ProTect app is still functional.

"I'm sorry. I didn't mean to scare you," says the beggar, but I am up the stairs and in the building.

I lay on the sofa, head spinning, waiting for sleep. I post #badday and there is a wave of #sosorrys, #what'swrong?s, #poorbabys, Kitten pix, Puppy pix, Frowny faces, inspirational quotes, and #feels on my wall. An email pings in. It's from my mother. Subj: Opportunity/joys of motherhood. There's an attachment, an advertisement for a surrogacy firm.

#notreadymom. I need updates. I turn DreamWell, and (poof) I'm out, dreaming an archived file.

The shop is old. My grandfather picks up something large and square. Dust flies, and I sneeze. "I remember these. My grandfather had these," he says chuckling. "Watch this." He pulls a black circle from the rectangle, puts it on something and flips a switch. The circle spins around and around. There's a noise like fingernails on wood. Then, music starts. There's no digital fixing, no lyrical translation, no tempo control; it's scratchy and all treble, the woman's voice is too shrill and in language that I don't understand. The song melancholy but joyous, sober but whimsical, flawed but... (poof) DreamWell pulls me into the next archived file. But there's something about the song, and I want to linger, to listen. DreamWell won't let me. Dwelling in files leads to obsession, and obsession leads to bad sleep, and bad sleep leads to low levels of something or other. LifeCoach works in concert with DreamWell and I'm pulled into the next archived file, then the next and the next, until I wake up in the morning, fully refreshed.

I roll off of the sofa, LifeCoach playing a light piano ditty in the background. "You have 165 new notifications, none of them urgent," it says. "Have patience, you can check the notification underway to work. For now, enjoy the perfect morning." I look out the window. Sun glints off of a pristine layer of snow coving my Art Deco wonderland.

#snow #newyork1950s #pureperfection

ProGusto has huevos rancheros ready and waiting in the kitchen.

AllGourmet level 5, #wow #pureperfection #timeforwork

Opening the door, I see people passing on the sidewalk, their feet leaving no impressions in the immaculate whiteness. I listen to the virgin snow, crunch, crunch, crunching beneath my feet as I walk down the stairs. It's the only sound in this muted, winter wonderland, and...

And something is missing, something that was here yesterday, but not today.

Opera music.

I find the crisply painted fire hydrant tucked into a corner of the alcove.

"Hello?" I say. It doesn't respond. "The snow is beautiful. Why aren't you singing today?" I ask. The hydrant remains silent. There's something wrong. It should be singing, moving, doing something.

"Hey," I say. "Hey?"

"Everything alright?" interrupts a voice from above me.

*Ping – *Juan da Silva Torrão, 47, lives in apartment 12J.*

He peers down into the alcove at me. I know what he's thinking.

#losingit #crazy

"Yeah. I just dropped something," I say.

"Okay," he says and walks down the stairs, foot prints disappearing as he goes.

The fire hydrant remains still, just sitting there as if frozen stiff.

Frozen stiff.

But it's not that cold, is it?

"Heart rate increasing, blood pressure rising. Time for a break," says LifeCoach. It starts playing a light piano ditty again. *The best choice is to just walk away. Don't get involved*, I think. *Just call the city. They'll send someone out in a jiffy to pick it up.*

It...

I take a step away from the fire hydrant.

Crunch, goes my foot into the immaculate white sheet.

A second. Crunch.

Five more. Crunch, crunch, crunch, crunch, crunch. I turn. My footprints are gone. There's only virgin snow between the fire hydrant and me. No trail of incrimination. I could leave now. When I come home later, (poof) the problem will simply disappear as readily as my footsteps.

"Blood pressure..."

I interrupt LifeCoach. Is he really frozen or just acting? Is this some pity game he's playing to get free food? Before yesterday, I didn't know he existed. But now I've seen. Now I know what's in that corner, cold and not moving. Oh God.

#terriblebadnogoodstupidstupidstupididea

But I have to.

As iPerceive shuts down, sunlight turns to shadow, pure snow turns to trodden slush and the silent hydrant turns to a shivering man, curled under a blanket in the only dry corner, and I...

#waitaminute

Shivering?

He's alive?

"Your heart rate is..." I interrupt LifeCoach and run to him.

"Hey..." I say. I've forgotten his name. He looks at me.

*Ping – Sergeant Steven Johnson

"Hey Steven," I say. "You're freezing," He nods. "You need help." He nods. "Okay, okay, okay, okay," I say.

"Epinephrine and norepinephrine critical. Anxiety is a health hazard. Relax, put your feet up. Imagine a happy place," says LifeCoach and starts a steel-drum-Caribbean ditty.

"Go to hell," I say, but the steel-drum ditty keeps playing. Sergeant Johnson's eyes widen. "No, no, no, not you. Don't go to hell. I was talking to LifeCoach," I say.

"L-l-l-i-i-f-f?" he stammers.

"Never mind," I say. But I still don't know what to do.

*Ping – *Treatment of hypothermia. Bring the victim to a warm place. Remove wet clothing. Wrap the victim in a blanket. Bring the victim a warm drink...*

#thankgodforwikisearch

I drape Sergeant Johnson over my shoulder and retch, twice. I've never smelled anything like him. My knees buckle as I take the first stair. I take the next two with my hand on the concrete.

Three stairs up, I hear:

"Lauren, I was just going by on my way to the office." I turn. Who is this bald man speaking to me? "Listen, I wanted to talk to you," he says. "I was able to catch the tail end of the action, but we missed out on most of the profit from the merger yesterday."

*Ping – *Rick Stock. Business Associate. Twitter: @rickstock538*

#OMG.

It's Rick, but it's not Rick. It's like Rick's chubby older brother.

"Okay, yeah. The merger," I grunt. Why doesn't he offer to help?

"Well, the problem is that this mistake is probably going to cost the company a pretty penny. This might be reflected in your bonus and..." I stumble. He cocks his head, "Is this a bad time?"

"I think that I need another day off," I say. Rick peers at the homeless man on my shoulder, opens his mouth and then closes it.

"Alright," he finally says. "It's your bonus, not mine." He turns to go and then stops. "Just out of curiosity, is this some kind of modern art or something?"

"Modern art?" I say, the steel-drum ditty in my head still going de-dada, da-da-da, do-do-do-do-do, de-de da-da-da.

"The fire hydrant," he says pointing at my shoulder.

"Oh, yeah," I say. "Modern art."

"You know that there's a new neo-perfectionist exhibit that you might be interested in. It's over on... (*Ping) ...Kinnickinnic Avenue," he says.

"Great, I'll check it out," I say.

75

"Alright," he says. "Enjoy your day off. See you tomorrow." Then, he trots down the slushy, dark sidewalk, cheerily whistling the same steel-drum-Caribbean ditty playing in my head.

Inside, I put Sergeant Johnson on the sofa.

*Ping – *Remove wet clothing. Wrap victim in a blanket.*

I do what WikiSearch tells me to. It's, well...unpleasant.

*Ping – *Bring victim a warm drink.*

I run to the kitchen. AutoBev pours a nice cup of, water?

#huh?

I asked for hot cocoa. Okay then, tea.

It's water.

Coffee = water.

Mulled wine = water.

Merlot = water.

Beer = water.

Coco loco = water.

Vodka? Water.

Talk about timing. My AutoBev is broken. I'm halfway through a message to the repair department when it hits me.

iPerceive on.

Suddenly, the kitchen is a gustatory wonderland, full of multicolored hot/cold/sweet/bitter/fizzy/flat/flamboyant drinks. I sip the vodka.

#burnssogood

I gulp it down, the whole cup. It's exactly what I need right now. There's a pleasant tingling in my stomach and fingers. My head drifts off like a balloon.

"Excuse me?" I hear from the other room.

iPerceive off. My head is clear as a bell.

Hmm...

On, buzzed.

Off, sober.

On, off, on, off, on/off/on/off/on/off.

"Hello?" calls Sergeant Johnson.

"Just a minute," I call back, grabbing the hot cocoa/water. Oh yeah, it's not even warm. It gets dumped in the disposal. I run to the bathroom, shove the cup under the showerhead and hope. Yes! It's warm.

#thankgod

Sergeant Johnson is sitting on my sofa, shivering. I hold out the cup and he takes it.

"Thank you," he says. "There's no need to panic. I'll be fine. I've seen worse." He looks at me, and sees me shaking worse than he is. "Really, I'll be fine," he adds.

"Look," I say. "This isn't a free ride. You can stay and get warm. I'll even get you something to eat, but then you have to go somewhere else."

"Where?" he says.

"I don't know. I'll find for you a place at a shelter or something. Is there anything else I can do for you right now?" I say.

"Yes," he says. "Tell me your name."

#impossible

He must not have any apps. Not even a rudimentary like iDentify.

"Lauren Van Kamp," I say.

"Thank you Ms. Van Kamp," he says and then lies back down on the sofa.

While he sleeps, I throw his clothes in the WashAll, setting it high enough to remove pain. While they dry, I InComp the city shelter. (Poof) Suddenly I'm standing in a concert hall sized room. It's stacked from floor to ceiling with occupied beds.

#cordwood

"Hello," says a worker. He's grey-haired and has bags under his eyes. iDentify tells me his name. I ask him if there's a free bed. He says no. I offer a small bribe. He says no. I offer a moderate bribe. "That's enough to afford LifeCoach. It looks like you could use it," I say. He laughs, then says that it doesn't matter how much I offer. The shelter is full. He clarifies:

#atcapacity

#wayovercapacity, actually. He takes me outside and shows me a crowd of hundreds of people. They're all waiting for a meal.

When did this happen?

*Ping – *Poverty has been on a steady incline since...*

I interrupt WikiSearch. This is another one of those things that I really don't need to know. Why haven't I seen this before? I flip iPerceive on.

A flock of storks...

#jesuschrist, that's why.

I flip iPerceive off. "I'm sorry, but there's nothing I can do," says the grey-haired man.

"Goodbye," I say, hanging up and shaking my head.

Sitting in my living room, I bury my head in my hands. LifeCoach tells me of my serotonin levels, suggest a day at the spa, offers wonderful holidays, real and virtual, and tells me that my self-satisfaction levels have dropped 452%, in a single hour. They're the lowest since I have gotten the app. I can't think, so I shut it off. I'd give anything for an #operasingingfirehydrant, for my #newyork1950s, for my #pureperfection, to forget.

I search the Dsense corp app store. There it is: GuiltFree. It promises to erase most of the last two days, but it's out of my price range. Maybe with my bonus...

#poop

I missed the merger, which means goodbye bonus.

✳

For lunch, my ProGusto cooks filet mignon with mashed potatoes. The two dishes are actually some type of grey protein slurry, just with different consistencies.

Sergeant Johnson is up and back in his clothes. He's in a good mood and wolfs the protein slurry down like it really is filet mignon. I turn on iPerceive and pick at my food while watching the crisply painted fire hydrant across the table from me. It's not moving, but the food slowly disappears.

The fire hydrant starts singing. "Huh," I say, turning iPerceive off.

"Is it supposed to be cold tonight?" he asks.

Very cold, but I don't tell him that. It's one of those things that he doesn't need to know. Instead, I say:

"There's no room at the shelter."

"Yeah," he says.

"And I can't keep you here," I say.

"I know," he says. He finishes his meal, gets up and slowly walks to the door, dragging his feet. He opens the door, turns and says, "Thank you." Then he smiles, scarred lip peeling back to reveal missing and rotten teeth. And there's something about the smile. It's not ugly. It's like the song, the one from my DreamWell archive, the one my grandfather played on the disc in the antique shop, melancholy but joyous, sober but whimsical, flawed but... real, something that I could touch, something I could feel, something created, existing only for a moment, shared between two human beings. It's not perfect; it's beautiful. Sergeant Johnson turns and leaves, shutting the door behind him.

I sit on the couch thinking about Sergeant Johnson. I play with iPerceive, flipping it on, turning it off, turning it back on, then back off. On, off, on, off, on/off/on. Now I'm at the door, now outside; now it's snowing again, cold and getting colder. I turn iPerceive off. I follow muddy tracks in the virgin snow.

Nathan Susnik is a medical writer who lives with his family near Hanover, Germany. His fiction has appeared in or is forthcoming from markets such as Cast of Wonders, Grievous Angel: Urban Fantasist, and Gallery of Curiosities. For more information, follow him on Twitter @NathanSusnik or visit his website www.nathansusnik.wordpress.com.

Apocalypse Beta Test Survey

Gregg Chamberlain

Greetings, **gentlebeing**, or whatever current alternative non-gender-specific address form is acceptable, and please excuse this interruption of your dream-state as we at Armageddon Inc. – where our motto is "The Horsemen are *always* ready to ride!" – ask you to consider taking part in a new project, inasmuch as our psychological profile indicates you may be someone with the potential interest and inclination to be part of a select subjects group to assist us in the beta-test of our new designer doomsday line of product services, which we are planning to introduce given the overwhelming popular appeal of the recent Mayan Calendar crisis, though this time we can assure one and all that every possible glitch is worked out to avoid a repeat of that fiasco, and also we can now offer a wide choice of cataclysms that will fulfill any apocalyptic fantasy, featuring such perennial favourites as: World War Three, with or without the atomic orbital bombardment option, along with ecological catastrophe, nuclear winter, solar flares or a full speeded-up expansion of the sun, plus we have a plethora of pandemic possibilities, and a new selection of current cutting-edge fads like robotic revolution, the biblical Judgment Day or other theological visions of doom like the Norse Ragnarok, complete with the Fimbul Winter, or, for the more intellectually-inclined, total global economic chaos, and, of course, we do have traditional fan favourites like alien invasion along with both a standard and a deluxe version zombie apocalypse, and all of these have a 100-per cent satisfaction guarantee with this no-risk trial offer or Armageddon Inc. promises to restore your space-time continuum to its current steady-state setup, minus an acceptable minimum of collateral damage or change based on our certified accounting department's calculations, and so before we return you to your theta-rhythm REM session, please take a nano moment to consider and take quick advantage of this exclusive, one-time-only, unique opportunity, our operators are standing by ready for your virtual signature on the contract, so be the first in your demographic to end the world before someone else beats you to it, and please note this offer may be void, prohibited or subject to certain restrictions on some planes of the multiverse, and with that cautionary note we thank you for your time and attention and if you will just submit yourself now to our customer survey satisfaction scan, totally painless we assure you, then we will once again thank you for your cooperation, wishing you good luck, and a nice life, however it might end.

Gregg Chamberlain lives in rural Ontario, Canada, with his missus, Anne, and their cats, who let the humans believe they are in charge. With more than four dozen short fiction credits, including three with *Shoreline of Infinity*, Gregg looks forward to retirement and writing more stories about worlds both weird and wonderful.

Published in *Shoreline of Infinity 9*

Little Freedoms

Ephiny Gale

The room is cylindrical, metal, no doors or windows. Nine of us stand in a circle, not touching, but spread your arms and you'd hit someone. I think I could lie flat in here without brushing the walls, but not by much.

The ceiling hatch above us locks shut with a scrape. We examine faces, muscles, body fat. I've seen six of these women before; two are complete strangers. We do not trade names or origin stories. We go around the circle and we say what we miss most from the outside:

Chocolate, Music, Flowers, Cigarettes, Hot Chips, Internet, Guns, Privacy.

I am Hot Chips. Privacy says hers while staring mournfully at the circular grate in the floor, and I think *oh, she must be new*.

When I was brand new I'd said "My Dog" thinking that was safe, and someone had laughed – not unkindly – and said, "Jeez, at least say your bitch."

The girl to my right asks, "So where are we going?" and there's a flurry of overconfident suggestions from those I assume got in through the physical trials. On the metal floor, every little step sounds like the smack of a frying pan. None of these women can know which terrain we're headed to. We've been told *You Must Not Assault One Another*, otherwise their disagreement may have turned violent.

Four of us are keeping our mouths shut, including me. I assume we're the four who got in the other way – 'The Lottery' – though it's not random at all. How much can you give up in a month? Food, sleep, shelter, dignity?

When there's a lull in the argument, Privacy points out a dollar-sized hole in the centre of the ceiling, releasing a single drop of water every two seconds, which falls through the middle of our tiny room and down through the floor grate. "Maybe we're not going anywhere," she says.

This is met with the obligatory smirks and laughter. Still, what feels like about twenty minutes has passed and nothing has happened, and many of us are fiddling with our shirt buttons, our fingernails, with the black bracelets locked on each of our wrists ("WIN YOUR FREEDOM" printed in Helvetica, light grey).

Once about thirty minutes have passed, there's an ascending chime like *the 7:15 train has been delayed* and a strip around the top of the cylinder hisses into pixelated life: *YOU MUST NOT FIDGET.* It's lit up for a couple of seconds, and then the same chime plays in *descending* order and it's gone.

There is laughter again, the most there's been, but now everyone's hands are motionless at their sides, or on their hips, or clasped in front of them. "This the big endurance test?" calls someone with muscles. "What a fucking piece of piss!"

Of course, when you're not allowed to do something you instantly need to do it a hundred times as much. My scalp, which felt fine seconds ago, prickles as if covered in lice. Itches blister down the sides of my neck, my wrist, above my eye. I trap my hands between the wall and my bottom and try to distract myself.

The others are arguing over whether this is the real challenge or not. I can see them flinching and wriggling every so often, as if to shrug off a troublesome insect. I am concentrating on my breathing.

My newfound desire to scratch my nose is shocking. If someone else raked their nails down my face, that wouldn't break the rules, would it? I am not desperate enough to share this secret yet.

The bug-eyed blonde on the floor – Flowers, I think, and maybe Melinda – starts complaining quietly about how much it feels like spiders are crawling over her skin. She knows a lot about spiders, too; she mentions several different breeds and the technical terms for the different segments of their legs. The others keep telling her to shut up, but Flowers keeps going, staring catatonically and moaning about rubbing her whole body against tree bark.

Eventually a girl with orange dreadlocks looks acutely nauseous, hauls Flowers up by the collar and raises her free hand in a fist. Flowers gasps and her eyes bug out like one of those goldfish.

At the last moment the fist uncurls and morphs into a middle finger salute instead.

Released, Flowers sinks back into the wall and smiles bashfully – "I'm sorry, Chocolate, did I upset you?" – but then her eyes darken and there's no confusion as to her innocence. When Chocolate turns her back, Flowers is up like a shot, parting the orange dreadlocks and blowing a single definitive breath on the back of Chocolate's neck.

It's more than enough. Chocolate leaps a foot in the air, scratching her neck with her fingernails like she's trying to rip the skin off. A pitch-black, translucent arm reaches through the metal wall and closes around Chocolate's wristband, and the whole 5'10" of her is yanked out of the room before the floor has even stopping vibrating from her jump.

Silence from the eight of us in the slightly-more-spacious cylinder. My eyes float slowly across from where Chocolate disappeared to the grate where Flowers is standing.

She looks completely serious. "Piece of piss, right?" she says.

YOU MUST NOT STAND.

There is no doubt anymore. This is our endurance test, and it will get easier and easier to lose, and we will be in here for as long as it takes.

When the second instruction flashes up, accompanied by the chime, we all sink to the ground almost in unison. There's not enough room for everyone to stretch out their legs at once, which is cause for some squabbling, but a rough hierarchy soon establishes itself.

With their legs out: Guns, the pretty Asian with the high-pony, the first to pee over the grate; Music, an athletic black woman with a chin scar; Cigarettes, a white girl who looks almost plump compared to the rest of us; and Flowers, with her legs half-over all the others'.

It's not like you can get far away from Flowers in here, but I'm pleased she's not *right* next to me.

Privacy asks Flowers why she's so desperate to get out – does she have children outside? And there's less laughter than I'm expecting, but all I can think is *new, new, God, you're so new*. Flowers says it's none of their business, but isn't that so stereotypical, that a woman needs to be a mother to throw someone else under the bus – can't she just want to free herself more than some strangers?

The room actually seems to warm to Flowers after that. Privacy climbs carefully over the outstretched legs and crouches over the grate, tilting her head to catch the ceiling drips on her tongue. I glance around and see a few women silently calculating whether to stop her – if they can hold her down until she's no longer a threat of any kind – but no-one moves.

We take it in turns to crouch under the drip and almost drink enough. While I'm sitting there, hurting my neck and seizing up my limbs, someone yells, "No camels!" which means I'm done for now.

Two or three hours have passed and it must be dark outside. The girl to my right, Internet, who's said barely more than I have, presses her lips to my ear and says, "Help me with something and I'll make it worth your while." I study her bony face, dark eyes, freckles... And nod.

She smiles and holds up the shoelaces she's pulled free. We're all in new uniforms for this and I feel stupid for not registering the laces earlier. "I want to sleep," she whispers. "But I'm afraid I'll itch. Can you tie up my fingers?"

I thread the laces between her digits and knot them so her fingers stay apart, then tie her hands together with the excess length. Some of the other women make bondage jokes, and though I think a couple understand the actual purpose they're not sharing out loud.

"You'll scratch my nose?" I ask, and she does, one long, firm scratch down both sides with her awkward bundle of hands.

"That's the bonus," she says, but doesn't elaborate.

Internet props herself against me, back to back, hands in lap, and might be napping as far as I know. The others aren't yelling, exactly, but there's a lively discussion about whether it's like this every year. The losers aren't allowed to mention the competition afterward, and the winner never comes back, of course.

I couldn't sleep with all that noise.

At one point Flowers unbuttons her shirt, folds it neatly and tucks it under her bottom. Everyone stares at her bare chest with various degrees of subtlety, because there are *actual* flowers there – tattoos of orchids stretching from her waist to the top of one breast, purple and yellow like permanent bruises.

It should make her more vulnerable, but Flowers wears it like armour and the group seems to treat it as such.

In the wake of this, Guns leans over and sticks her tongue inside Privacy's ear, and Privacy lets out a horrified gasp but doesn't jump to her feet like Guns obviously wants her to. I wait to see if The Powers That Be consider this assault, but apparently not, and thankfully Guns doesn't follow it with anything more extreme.

A couple more hours pass without incident and the group seems to conclude that now, in the early stages, is a useful time to get some sleep. I've agreed since Internet slumped against my back, but I can't let my eyes close. I'm a violent sleeper, the kind that steals the covers and kicks shins and tosses like a suffocating fish.

Some of the other women get shoe laces tied around their fingers. One by one, threats are issued or goodnights whispered and eyelids shut around the circle. Then there's only Music, Flowers and me awake and staring at one another.

My legs are aching by now, and one of them has suffered pins and needles for the last half hour. I twist carefully on the floor and stretch my legs into the air in the middle of the circle, careful not to touch the sleepers. While I massage the feeling back into my calves, I can see Flowers grinning at me from the corner of my eye.

Flowers is making hand puppets at me. I can't tell what they are, exactly, but they change rapidly and are surprisingly animate. I force my face to stay blank, impassive. Eventually she cocks her head like *poor dumb bitch* and opens her mouth as if to scream.

Silence. She shuts her mouth again, then opens it and takes a deep breath.

More silence. She does this a third time, and it really looks like she's going to screw up her face and shriek, but Music shoves her own shirt in Flowers' mouth and ties it firmly behind her blonde head.

Flowers jerks against the wall and reaches up for the ties, picking at the knot for a second before realising that's an awful lot like fidgeting. She glares at Music for a straight hour after that, and Music stares back for a lot of it. Allowing your competition to sleep seems a strange tactic to me, but perhaps Music just hates Flowers. Or loves the silence. Or has a tiny, fragile alliance, like mine with Internet.

We sit there for a while longer until Flowers gradually retrieves her legs from the middle of the circle and picks her way, hunched and Gollum-like, over to me. She unfolds something navy and red-brown between us – her shirt, wet with menstrual blood – and manages to grin at me around her gag.

I open my mouth to protest, but she pivots to the girl on my left instead.

I realise I don't know this girl, and I don't remember the thing she misses most – I don't think I even heard it in the first place. And now Flowers is draping the bloody shirt over her head, and the wet part's all over her sleeping face.

Flowers sits back down and I'm frozen to the wall, and it's not like this is the worst thing I've ever seen, far from it, but it's so *silent* and *cold* and *easy* when getting here in the first place was so damn *hard*.

The ascending chime goes off, and it is *loud*.

Several things happen at once. No-name next to me wakes up with a face full of cotton and blood, and kind of a half-sob and staggers to her feet and gets dragged through the wall.

The rest are frantically blinking themselves awake and trying to focus on their new instructions, which, incidentally, read *YOU MUST NOT SLEEP.*

And Internet is struggling towards the grate, pulling down her pants awkwardly with her tied hands, and rocking back too far at the last moment...

She pees on everyone but me.

Internet sits back down and doesn't apologise, because what is there to say, and women don't generally pee in a 180-degree arc by accident.

There are shouts of outrage and swearing and clearly suppressed wriggling from the other prisoners. Privacy looks like she's going to throw up, and I expect her to throw in the towel at this point but she doesn't move.

Instead, Cigarettes is the one flailing and shaking her legs to try and get the piss off them, and bounding to her feet and the urine's running down her ankles and then there's a translucent hand around her bracelet and she's gone.

Guns, Privacy, Music and Flowers are all taking off their soiled shoes and trousers and I think I had better, too, so I don't draw attention to my relative cleanliness. They toss their trousers at Internet, who is soon sitting in a pile of dirty cotton, and their shoes in a cluster over the grate so they're not eliminated for actually battering the woman. Music mimes several different ways of ending Internet's life, includes slicing her jugular, wrists, hanging, stabbed in the guts... Music has her thumbs in her underwear and I think she might go and return Internet's 'favour' but Guns mouths "Later" and the room is silent for a bit.

Privacy has started crying in that way where the tears drop but the rest of your face looks normal. Guns leans over and licks them off her cheeks with some comment about water conservation. Through her makeshift gag, Flowers starts humming a familiar tune that I haven't heard for years and can't quite put my finger on. It's a children's song, one of those ones that keeps repeating over and over.

"It's that bear song," says Internet, slowly shifting the peed-on trousers away from her and onto the grate. And of course it is, that song about a bunch of bears in a bed and they all roll over and fall out one by one until it's just the little bear left and I've forgotten what happens then, if anything. Flowers is still humming and Guns calls her a sociopath.

And then there are six of us, and there's almost enough space to be comfortable, and there's wakefulness stretching before us like the desert – all the way to the horizon.

The cylinder is truly unpleasant now. The smell of drying urine is impossible to ignore, as is the hunger gnawing at my stomach. It's easy to imagine the hunger as a seventh person, expanding around us until she fills all the empty space. It's going to be one of us Lottery girls next, I'm sure, quitting just for the relief of a proper meal.

When the chime sounds again, the pile of trousers has moved and Privacy is squatting tenuously under the drip. Flowers scuttles along the floor and drags Privacy back towards the wall by her biceps, where Privacy flails and collides with Music in a muddle of limbs. Flowers claims the spot over the grate just as *YOU MUST NOT TOUCH* blinks to life above us.

I watch the conflict flash desperately over Music's face. There's barely time to extract herself, so instead she throws Privacy aside. Privacy's a tall woman so it has to be a big push, but the force slams Privacy's arms and forehead against the metal floor and there's no doubt about the pain involved.

The descending tone finishes and Music's bottom lip quivers. Then there's a hand around her wrist, and she sinks back into the wall like it's liquid and disappears.

Flowers is kneeling on the grate, head tipped back and catching the water happily on her gag. The ramifications of this slowly register: as long as we're not allowed to touch her, and as long as Flowers doesn't move, she's effectively cut off our water supply. None of us can reach it without standing or risking touching her.

"Fuck you, Melinda," says Guns, and we watch Privacy pick herself up like reassembling a doll. She isn't bleeding or crying, but there's a hardness to her face I haven't seen before. I suppose she might have a concussion.

"No-one would blame you for leaving," Guns tells her. "*That* kind of hurt – it's not part of the rules."

Privacy leans herself gingerly against the wall and doesn't answer.

"Alright," says Guns, now addressing everyone. "Just remember that this could be a lot worse. Forgotten what it's like outside? If you can't survive in here you'll have trouble out there. You can't die in prison."

Internet tucks her hands between her thighs. "You can die anywhere," she says.

And it's tempting. It's so tempting. How much I want to scratch, stand and stretch, drink and eat my fill, sleep and feel someone's hands on me. To recover those little freedoms. I have lost all sense of time in this place. *How long how long how long.*

My tired eyes rest on Flowers and an idea sparks.

For the first time since we were locked in here, I shift from my designated spot in the circle and crawl around to the opposite wall. Guns and Internet swing their legs over to accommodate me.

I peel a couple of pair of trousers from the soiled pile, trying to ignore their dampness, and tie both right legs together at the ankles; they'll stretch out to almost four legs' worth of length now. The knot is as secure as I can make it.

I keep hold of one end of the trouser-rope and slide the other end in Guns and Internet's direction. They both eye it for a second, and then Guns gives me the ghost of a smirk and picks up the cotton ankle I've offered. We pull the rope almost tight and it stretches neatly across the diameter of the circle.

Flowers still has her face to the sky and looks oblivious. I feel a delirious burst of satisfaction at the back of my skull.

Guns mouths *one, two, three* and then we swing the rope in an arc over Flower's head. It catches her mid-thigh and we hook it under her arms before she can retaliate. We jerk the rope backwards and up, and in a deliciously similar manner to what she did to Privacy, Flowers is yanked off the grate and pinned up against the wall.

For a moment Flowers seems frozen with terror, but I know her stillness is simply profound control of the game. She doesn't bash her feet against the floor. She doesn't try and untangle her arms; she will touch us if she does, and she will be disqualified. She contents herself by swivelling her head between Guns and myself, administering some of the most withering looks I've seen.

Internet and Privacy tie the last pairs of trousers together – Internet has to remove her own pair for an even number – and between the four of us we manage to tie Flowers' arms to her sides and her knees together. Then we take grateful turns under the drip. One of us could easily monopolise the water again, but there are still several shirts we can tie in knots, and no-one else wants to end up like Flowers.

A little while later, Privacy comes and leans next to me whilst Guns is drinking. "Tell me," she says. "Why no names? No back-stories? Just this one thing you miss. No-one explains properly."

I feel sweaty and self-conscious and exhausted. "I don't know," I mumble. "I guess because those first two don't matter in here. We're never getting the past back. But maybe it's not too much to ask, that one small thing you miss most. Maybe you can get that back, in another life."

I see her nod from the corner of my eye. "Like hot chips?"

I shrug. "It seems a reasonable thing to want."

We smile at each other, just a little, and for a moment the competition is a fraction easier.

Then Guns rocks back onto her ass. She stares at the ceiling – the dry ceiling, the ceiling that is no longer dripping – and we are plunged into the next phase with no ceremony whatsoever.

If time had seemed unwieldy before, now it feels utterly amorphous. Logically, we can't really have been stuck in the cylinder for all that long, but it's suddenly difficult to imagine life outside these few cubic meters. I fight the nearly-overwhelming urge to leave just to reassure myself that other places – other situations – exist.

And even with my churning hunger and sickening exhaustion, it is so *dull* in here. No-one wants to talk without access to water, and this test seems to have reduced itself to *who can sit here the longest.* I wish I was smart enough to think of a way to eliminate the others – I could even justify it as putting them out of their misery – but I can't come up with a thing.

Finally, Flowers starts crashing her heels against the floor, causing great thumps to reverberate throughout the room. They're slow, methodical; no one could accuse her of fidgeting. The others glance amongst themselves to see if they can stop her somehow, but it's not like they can hogtie her. And I am oddly grateful for the interruption, the un-ignorable sound, the vibrations which run up my stiff legs. I feel a rush of absurd affection for Flowers.

But Flowers doesn't stop the banging. Guns and I end up curled on the floor, shirts cushioning our heads and hands muffling our exposed ears. Privacy and Internet seem happier sitting, though there's barely room for them to do otherwise. Guns has two Asian characters tattooed on the underside of her wrists, and I spend a good half hour or so trying to deduce their meaning.

I could ask, of course, but that would ruin the game.

Flowers goes on for so long her heels must be swollen with orchid-bruises. I don't know what makes her snap in the end. But one moment she's bashing the floor, the next she's rolling into Internet, whose jaw drops like Flowers has just slid a knife into her gut.

They leave silently, simultaneously.

I guess Flowers decided she couldn't win. I would've thought she'd take Guns with her, but then Internet's pee has pressed against her skin for the last few eternities. There's a half-dried bloodstain where Flowers was sitting.

I am very, very lucky.

There are just three of us left. Not at all the last three I was expecting. My brain's not working so well anymore. I have the sudden image of the cylinder as a time capsule, and someone digging up our skeletons in a hundred years.

The sign flashes *YOU MUST NOT TALK*, and clearly, no shits are given.

Something flares in my aching chest. Only two more to beat.

I could actually win.

The next part is a small lifetime. I allow myself to fantasise about my possible freedom. Will they let me sleep and wash and dress before throwing me out, or just take me directly outside, starving and thirsty and half-naked?

I will strip 'til I'm bare and stand in the sun. I will stare at an uninterrupted horizon. I will lick salt and spices from my fingers. I will never take anything for granted again.

The ascending chime, and then *YOU MUST NOT MOVE*.

Frantic movements as we all try and stretch out onto our backs without touching each other.

We succeed.

Privacy doesn't have anything between her head and the floor; Guns and I will be much more comfortable.

And for the first few minutes, this is better than the nothingness. I am concentrating on not moving. Not moving a millimetre. Of course, no-one can concentrate forever.

My shoulder blades press down against the metal.

I just have to last longer than the others.

I assume the rules are the same as Sleeping Lions or Dead Fish, those games we played as a kid when the adults wanted ten minutes of peace: breathing and blinking are still allowed. We're on our backs so we can still read the pixelated sign, though I can't imagine

93

how our freedom could be restricted further. Our eyes have to be open for that, and so we have to be able to blink.

I think of myself as a corpse. As a mannequin. I am acutely aware of every protesting part of my body. I think of the time I needed my wisdom teeth out, but the teeth were too close to my nerves, and if I'd moved even a millimetre during surgery I would have permanently lost the feeling in my jaw.

So I didn't have that surgery, but I can do this. I am made of fucking *steel*.

There are times when I think *I want to die, I want to die*, but I don't move. I will not move. Not when I've come this far.

A small sound whistles to my right. Guns really must have been comfortable, because she's *snoring*. And then, of course, she's not there anymore.

I think of Privacy. If this was a kinder world, I would sacrifice myself for her, or she would sacrifice herself for me. And things would be hopeful and uplifting and we'd know we'd done the right thing.

But this is not that world.

The chime comes again, for the last time, and it says *YOU MUST NOT BREATHE.*

I hold my breath on the second last note.

I don't know if I can do this. I was a decent swimmer, once upon a time, but that was years ago.

I stare at the ceiling and bite my tongue.

The pressure is building in my stomach, my nose, my throat. It feels like my face is an overfilled balloon, about to burst. Heat crawls up my neck. I think I can see Privacy from the corner of one eye: I just need to hold on longer than her. Just a millisecond longer. Then I can breathe.

Privacy is still lying there. My vision is blurring.

It's involuntary. I can't- I won't-

I take a breath and cry out. It's a tiny cry. There is no energy for tears. My whole body is shaking. I have lost. I will not get to leave. All that, so much for nothing.

I keep expecting to feel a shadowy hand on my wrist, but seconds pass and it never does.

I struggle to my knees. Privacy must know she's won, but she's just lying there. Still motionless.

I can't even see her chest rising. *The head blow?*

I crawl across the room and press my fingers to her neck, hold them under her nose.

She really did stop breathing.

I slouch over the grate and stare at nothing in particular. It's awful, it's a tragedy, but mostly all I can think is *I've won, I've won by default* and laugh and laugh inside my head, and it feels like my skin's just peeled off my body and I've been given a fresh, light, clean one.

Beside me, a large panel slides open in the wall and the prison warden steps through, flanked by her usual guards.

"I won," I say, sounding like a small child and not caring.

"No," says the warden. "Geraldine won."

Is that really Privacy's name, I think, numb. *It doesn't fit her.*

I blink at them, feeling like the adults have come home to my messy playroom. "She's dead," I say. "I won."

"You took a breath before she did. You knew the rules. And she's already received her prize; she has her freedom."

The wind is knocked out of me. The guards pick me up and carry me out. I cannot move. I cannot speak. Slowly, I adjust to the world outside the cylinder.

Next year, I think. Next year I'll win.

And in the meantime, little freedoms.

Ephiny Gale has written more than two dozen published short stories and novelettes, which have appeared in publications including *GigaNotoSaurus*, *Daily Science Fiction*, and *Aurealis*.
Much of her short fiction has recently been collected in *Next Curious Thing*. She is also the author of several produced stage plays and musicals.

Published in *Shoreline of Infinity 10*

The Brat and the Burly Qs

David Perlmutter

1.

It seemed like the usual scenario: fly in, tell the bad guy he sucks, stomp him up a bit, and "save the day", as they put it. But there's always a sort of complication involved before you can go ahead and restore order, and this was a bit more unusual than most.

First, allow me to introduce myself, as it's likely we've never met or spoken before this time, right?

My given name, such as it is, is Precious XY-300. The reason being is that I come from a planet (*yes*, I'm an *alien*) where the natives have half their bodies made out of metal on account of our evolution to the climate – you don't see it on me so much 'cause I painted my mechanical parts so that they'd look more "human". I'm here on your Earth, and going under the cover name Precious O'Reilly, on account of some skullduggery in my homeland I'd rather not go into now. Too painful. The point is, I ended up in your solar system, and I now fight crime etc. within it as the Brat. That accounts for the "B" on my shirt, in case you were wondering.

Now, you might *also* be wondering what a "three year old girl", blonde haired, blue eyed, wearing a blue wool jacket, white skirt and boots, and the aforementioned shirt, is doing here in a bar unaccompanied, and drinking a beer. Well, let's get something straight, pal. I'm *not* a three year old girl! I can pass as one, as you'll soon see, but, in all other respects, I am an *adult*. Everyone on my planet is the same, diminutive size as me through youth and adulthood. Anyone over 4 feet tall is considered as much of a freak of nature as someone who weighed 400 pounds or more would be amongst you guys. Still, people see me as a little girl and treat me like it. Until I open my mouth or throw a punch at them, that is.

Sorry for the info dump, but it's necessary to understand the story I'm gonna tell ya. I don't want the good readers of "Super Heroics Illustrated" getting the wrong idea about me, after all. And it's a sign of good faith on your part that you can keep that thing going, considering how many of us don't want to talk to you. But my friends say you're legit, so I guess I can trust you. Up to a point!

Anyhow, this is what happened on Mars:

2.

I was alerted to the situation by my associates in the Interplanetary League Of Girls With Guns (referring to our collective Herculean musculature, but, in my case, also to my built-in weaponry). The five of us, as soon as we knew of each other's existence, struck up a gentlelady's agreement that we'd each patrol a particular sector of the universe, and wouldn't interfere with each other's business unless things got too hot for us to handle alone. (Like it does, once in a while.) Anyway, they told me that that son of a bitch Machine Gun Steinberg had managed to escape from his confinement on Earth, overpowered the nearest set of security guards, and re-established his burlesque business in the ugly imitation French Quarter they set up in New New Orleans, so named as it's at the extreme southern tip of the newly terraformed Earth colony in the shadow of Olympus Mons.

This rattled my coils. Who do you think was responsible for putting that guy in jail in the first place? Me, that's who! And thus, by the informal ILGWG rules, I had to put him *back* there. Not that I *minded* that!

Steinberg, as you probably know, was the man who single-handedly revolutionized the "art" of "burlesque" (i.e. stupid young humans taking their clothes off) by managing to create pliable mechanical strippers for the first time. Or, I should say, *part* mechanical. He scurried around human graveyards, finding undecomposed human body parts, and then had them welded together with a variety of mechanical features to make them…. interesting enough for the "patrons" of the "art". Electronic legs, remote controlled boobs, and so on. Naturally, the girls have automatic brains, so that they only do as they're told all the time. No free-thinking real human woman I know would actually get involved with that crap unless they were really desperate for cash.

However, he made money. And aroused the ire of feminists, besides. And, ultimately, I had to step in and destroy his assets before anything apocalyptic happened. 'Cause he was actually getting women coming to him for jobs, women who wanted a mechanical transplant added to their natural bodies. They were lining up outside his club for work on their own free will. Jeez!

Thus, I found myself flying to Mars. (Yeah, *that* type of flying, of course. I'm a superhero, after all.) That John Gray fellow was damn right when he said men came from Mars. Imagine Texas, or better yet, your average big city downtown on a Saturday night, and that's exactly what Mars has become ever since the creation of synthetic water allowed that liquid to flow through those mythical canals and make Ray Bradbury's dreams a reality. Naturally, you have settlements that resemble the Wild West in the days when it was actually *was* wild. Like New New Orleans. Ugly as hell, and not the place that even a three year old girl can walk around for fear of having her feminine virtue permanently immolated.

Not that I'm one of *those*.

3.

I made New New Orleans in good time, and was soon in the ugly imitation French Quarter, with Martian natives coerced into adopting phony Creole and Cajun *patois* and strutting around like they owned the place. (Two words: *em*-barrasing!). I was soon able to find Steinberg's, owing to the giant neon sign displaying both his name and the backside of a giant woman with outlined 3D boobs.

As Fat Albert and the Cosby Kids would say- *no class*!

I walked to the front door and started to put on my best three year old girl act, with voice and gestures to match, in hopes the bouncer would let me in.

"Is my *mommy* in there?" I piped up.

The guy apparently couldn't *see* me, on account of the fact that he actually started walking around and asking "Who said that?" I wasn't surprised. With his gut being so big, he probably hadn't seen his own feet for some time.

In any event, I repeated my question, in a shriller and more pleadingly desperate tone. That time, he knew I was there and looked at me.

"You *want* somethin', lil' girl?" he asked me, contemptuously.

"I wan' my *mommy*!" I said, tears coming to my cheeks.

"She ain't here!"

"Mommy said wait out here while she takes her clothes off to earn money for her meth…."

"Ain't none of my concern, kid."

"An'…..An'……I'm so all alone…..an' scared….'cause Daddy gonna beat her up if he found she spen' th' rent money on *meth* again…."

"You hard of hearin', *brat*? I *said* she ain't *here*!"

Well, that *did* it! I'm a brat, all right, but only with a capital B, not a small one. I shucked my coat off, hardened my expression, grabbed his ankle with my super-powered mechanical right arm, and made a fist with my organic left one.

"Listen, buddy!" I exclaimed in my natural voice. "You might think I'm *a* brat, but I'm *The* Brat! You *understand?* I'm the most powerful three year old in the universe, and I can knock you *six ways from Sunday* if I take a *dIs*-like to you. Now, your *employer* is a wanted fugitive from Earth, and I intend to take him back where he belongs. You *dig* that, MOTHERFUCKER?"

Having said my peace, I threw the dude over my shoulder, and he ran away from me like the beaten dog he was. There now remained only Steinberg, and I proceeded to enter his establishment to silence him.

4.

I brushed through the informal anterooms and entered the main ballroom chamber of Steinberg's joint. It was typical Wild West bedlam: half-mechanical girls parading around in next to nothing on the stage, or sat on the exclusively male patrons' tables, chairs and laps. They, of course, were doing everything possible to encourage the drinking, dancing and stripping done by the girls. I, however, would not.

"*STEINBERG!*" I screamed, with fists clenched.

Everything went dead silent, and everyone looked at me, like in Western movies when the bad guy walks into the saloon looking for the hero. That's the way it was, only in this case, the hero came looking for the villain.

I walked over to a table of miscreants, who were drunk, like they usually are.

"Get out," I drawled humorlessly.

"Come *on*, man!" one of them said. "We just wanna…"

I gave them no chance to explain. I pressed a few invisible buttons on my mechanical arm. The hand temporarily raised, and a jet of flame burst out and destroyed the chairs they had been sitting on. (They moved to escape it, of course.) Then my hand snapped back into place.

"I *SAID* 'GET OUT'!"

The men – all of them – got out of the building, leaving only the puzzled looking girls. Then Steinberg entered, having been in the back.

"Jesus Christ," he shouted. "How many times have I gotta tell ya…."

His blood turned cold and his words stopped as soon as he saw me.

"What the hell are *you* doing here?" he said. "I didn't think you supes had any authority off of Earth…"

"You poor, dumb, delusional *putz*!" I shot back. "Don't you realize I can be anywhere I want, any *time* I want? And that means I can collar your deluded *ass* any time I want, too! You disappoint me, Steinberg. My fellow heroes have much more imposing, threatening, *masculine* foes to deal with, but *I* have to settle for a third rate Woody Allen impersonator!"

He cursed me violently, up and down, in Yiddish, thinking I didn't know the language, and, thus, would not know my honor had been insulted. But I *did* know the language, and fluently at that. This I demonstrated not only repudiating what he had just said about me, but by further compromising his own limited integrity.

"Bah!" he said, switching back to English. "It's time I was rid of you. Burly Qs!"

At this moment, all of Steinberg's cyborg automatons came to attention, and stood stiff as soldiers in a line in front of me.

"Steinberg," I asked rhetorically, "are you *kidding* me? You know perfectly well that I…."

"….am stronger and more powerful than any other *goyim* child of your age in the universe, on account of your alien birth and mechanical 'enhancements'." He interrupted me, reproducing my usual intro spiel to opponents (but adding the *goyim* to spite me.) "*Oy*! Do I *ever* know that! But that's why I had the Avicenna Development Corporation fix this lot up for me – so I could *defend* myself from you!"

"Avicenna?" I spat on the ground to indicate my contempt for them. "Those *hacks*? They couldn't build a decent robot without *killing* people to do it!"

"You won't think so once the girls get through with you."

"I doubt that they have much on them. Just like *you*."

"*Fine,* girlfriend! You *asked* for it. Burly Qs- *attack!*"

The girls shed their humanized exteriors to reveal guns, weapons and ammo encased in their hair, eyes, teeth, noses, hands, arms, legs, feet and even their you-know-whats. And, at their master's command, they proceeded to attack me *en masse*.

I responded by employing my own weapons to fire at them, though I did so more strategically, dropping, rolling and tucking (like my opponents probably did onstage) to avoid their weapons, and then staggering them with shots from my arm-gun when I saw a chance. That allowed me to pick a few of them off, and they exploded, inert, into mounds of useless flesh and metal within seconds.

The three remaining half-mechanical bitches ganged up on me from behind. One encased me in a powerful bear hug I couldn't break, another bounced out a mechanical net, which the first one threw me into and tied up above me, and then the third one, while I was trying to open the net at the top, did a Spider-Man with her wrist and shot some piping hot, bubbling grey liquid at my mechanical side. I wasn't able to move in time, so it covered me all over. Holy shit, did it *sting*!

"JESUS *CHRIST*!" I ejaculated, in the midst of my pain.

Now, as I am normally invulnerable to the works of Man, this came as quite a shock to me. I soon reasoned what was going on as I saw my powerful mechanical arm give off sparks, shut down, and go limp, and my bionic right leg go likewise. Steinberg had, likely through his connections, managed to find a store of liquid mercury – the one material in the universe to which natives of my planet are vulnerable – and surreptitiously charged one of his robot-strippers with it to wound me. That he did, and soon as he did, the three of them took advantage of my reduced circumstances and started beating the shit out of me.

While I took their hits, I lamented my fate and beat myself up mentally.

What the hell am I gonna DO? I said to myself. My guns and weapons are gone. I've just got my body and my wits, and that might not be enough.

Yet that stereotypical minute of self-doubt existed for only a couple of seconds. I suddenly remembered what I *did* have. A *brain.* The mightiest weapon of them all. A brain will get you out of things even superpowers can't, if you use it and nurture it right like I do. Sure, I know that those cyborg types have brains, too, but they're *fake* brains, run on electrical impulses rather than natural nerve generators. No substitute.

This I showed them with the still active – and still powerful – left, organic side of my body. Once I had freed myself from their trap, I dislocated their mechanical parts from their organic ones. That being done, I caught Steinberg trying to make his exit out the back door.

"No, you fucking WON'T!" I snapped.

I overtook him, lifted him above my head, and threw him into one of the abandoned tables of the club. He was down and out.

I proceeded to give him the same ruminations on the brain I just gave you, as well as more profanity laced ones about how *important* the metal half of my body *is* to me, how he was going to personally pay cash money to replace every single part of me the mercury damaged, and how I was going to personally escort him back to Earth, and jail-after that. I particularly emphasized that he should STAY there if he did not want any more trouble.

"You got any PROBLEMS with that?" I concluded.

He didn't.

5.

Oops. My pager. I gotta go, man. Let me know when the story comes out. And, for *your* sake, it better be *flattering!*

David Perlmutter is based in Winnipeg, Manitoba, Canada. The holder
of an MA degree from the Universities of Manitoba and Winnipeg, and a
lifelong animation fan, he has published short fiction and essays in a variety of
publications. He is the author of *America Toons In: A History of Television Animation*
(McFarland and Co.), *The Singular Adventures Of Jefferson Ball* (Chupa Cabra
House) and *The Pups*

Incoming

Thomas Clark

Andy had just got off to sleep when it started again. It was getting to be every night now. He staggered out of bed, pulled his wax jacket on over his pyjamas. It could only have been three o'clock. Blearily, he stared at the Daedalian knots of his laces, tucked them down into the sides of his shoes. The close lights were broken, but the stairwell was already bright with open doors.

"Mornin, Mrs. McGraw," he shouted at the first door. Mrs. McGraw glowered at him, her weathered fist clasping shut her nightie like a brooch.

"Ah'll gie ye morning! It's a bloody disgrace, so it is," she said, "There's ma man daein mornins and he cannae get a wink o sleep."

"Ah ken, ah ken," Andy said, "Ah'm just away doon tae see aboot it."

"Aye, well, when ye see him ye can tell him fae me …"

The noise, a continual low hum which shook the windows in their settings, suddenly redoubled, driving out all competing sounds. As he passed down through the stairwell, Andy tried not to notice the faces that stared lividly at him from the cracks of doors, the horrific writhings of their silent mouths. By now the noise was so loud that his eyes quivered in their sockets, and the close had the freakish appearance of double exposed film, an art-house installation for the criminally insane. "Sorry, sorry, sorry," he found himself whispering as he shuffled past the doors, each framing a scene of suspended domesticity warped into something grotesque.

Outside, on the street, it was just as bad. Fractals of window-light pocked the low clear night, and the noise boomed through the narrow roads as they sunk towards the fields. As he walked along, Andy took a glance at the town hall spire. The clock was usually wrong, but it was certainly well past four. On the farms beyond Hawick, hired hands were already rising: Bulgarians and Poles who washed their faces in freezing water and listened with wonder to the sound, which could be heard as far as Branxholme Castle. It wasn't until the valleys towards Galashiels that the noise finally passed beyond the range of human hearing, although the Jedburgh dogs still whined, and the sheep in Selkirk bleated sympathy. No-one knew.

"It's not on, Andy, ah'm tellin ye," Johnny McEwan roared out of his window, "Ah'm on the phone tae the cooncil first thing. As if it's no bad enough UHRRRR"

Johnny threw his hands to his ears, but Andy knew from experience that nothing short of industrial grade ear muffs could block out this new noise: a long metallic shriek like a thousand rusty brakes. As the old man fell to his knees groaning, Andy pointed at an imaginary watch.

"Ah ken, Mr. McEwan, ah ken," he shouted, "Ah'm just away tae tell him. It's past a joke, this."

By the time Andy had turned the corner onto the high street, the noise had stopped, lingering only in the high arches of the town walls, like a trapped bird trying to get out. D-CON, who had never shown the slightest bit of interest in it before, was crouched down next to the 1514 Memorial, scanning its inscription raptly. Darkness once again had settled.

"Like butter widnae melt, eh," Andy said, "Whit's the game here then, pal? Whit's wae aw the noise?"

D-CON looked down at Andy with an immoderate start, as if only just noticing him.

"WHY ANDREW, I WAS …"

"Shh! Shh!" Andy whispered, the concrete shifting tectonically beneath his feet. The robot started again.

"APOLOGIES, ANDREW. WHAT NOISE?"

Andy screwed up his face.

"What noise? You got selective super-hearing all of a sudden? You're at it, big man. Ah've telt ye wance, ah've telt a hunner times – when it gets dark, folk are tryin to sleep."

"ANDREW, I CANNOT SLEEP."

"Name o God … Whit, you want me to sing you a lullaby?"

"I …"

"Ah'm jokin," Andy said hastily, "Ah ken whit you mean. But look, if you're no able tae sleep at night, can you no just dae whit everybody else does an watch the telly or somethin? Get any channel ye like wae aw that gear stickin oot yer heid. Ah mean … och, here we go."

A Volvo driving the wrong direction up the one-way street came to a sudden halt across the road. After a moment's struggle, a fat man with unkempt hair and a provost's chain over his nightgown wrangled his way out from under the steering-wheel and waddled over towards them. The backs of his slippers made a soft padding noise on the tarmac.

"Right, Andy! Whit's going on here? Giein ye any problems, is he?"

"Naw, Davie, it's just ..."

"This is no good enough, Andy. It's needing nipped in the bud, like. Bloody robot getting the run of the place. Honest tae God."

Davie squinted in D-CON's direction. There were marks on either side of his nose where his glasses normally sat. He shook his head.

"Nae wunner his name's C-CON. C-CON, is it! It's enough tae seeken onybody. Ah'm telling ye, Andy ..."

"His name's D-CON," Andy said, "Like Deacon Blue."

"Ah'm tellin ye, Andy," Davie continued, "Folk've just aboot had enough o this. D'ye have any idea how much it's costing us tae keep him?"

"Well, he's solar-powered, Davie, so ..."

"Solar power!" Davie spat, "In Hawick? That's a joke! He's suckin this toon dry. An as for ..."

"IF I FLEW INTO THE SUN," the robot interrupted, "I COULD RECHARGE TO FULL CAPACITY WITHOUT ..."

"Aye, that'll be shining bright!" Davie veered slowly round, lifting up his eyes rather than his head. "Efter aw the money we've spent, we're just gonnae let ye fly away! D'ye think ma heid buttons up the back or sowt? Fly away, he says!"

Davie shook his head again, as if it was the only point of articulation his body had. His arms were folded so high across his chest that his chin was almost resting on them, and he was breathing heavily. Andy cleared his throat.

"Look, Davie," he said, "We cannae have it both ways. If we want tae keep him to ourselves, that's fair enough, but somebody's got to foot the bill. That's just economics."

"Oh aye?" Davie said without looking at him, "Get that aff your da, did ye? Dead smart, your da. Dunno how he's only working in a chippy."

With one last glower at D-CON, Davie turned on his heel and walked back across the road. Andy, whose cheeks had become a lipstick pink, looked up at the robot and smiled awkwardly. He always forgot that D-CON did not have emotive facial expressions or, for that matter, emotions.

The provost's car coughed and spluttered back into life. Like the provost himself, it had been serving in its official capacity for as long as Andy could remember. With much uncomfortable to-ing and fro-ing, Davie squeezed an arm between his bulk and the door and jerkily rolled down the window.

"Oh, aye, and while ah remember," he said, "Where are we at wae they comet things?"

The robot stared up into the sky.

"REPORT. NEAR-EARTH OBJECTS OBSERVED. QUANTITY: THREE. VELOCITY: 110 KILOMETRES PER SECOND. TIME OF IMPACT: 4.2 DAYS. CURRENT VISIBILITY FROM EARTH: ZERO. EXPECTED SURVIVAL RATE WITHIN IMPACT ZONE: ZERO. EXPECTED IMPACT ZONE: GALASHIELS."

Davie nodded in satisfaction.

"Right, that's a Wednesday then, eh? Ah'll let the bus drivers ken."

"Davie, d'ye no think ..."

"Not a chance! Forget it!" Davie said, "Where were they when *we* were the wans aboot tae get smashed intae bits? Couldnae look the other way quick enough then! For aw they kent oor goose was cooked, an they never even lifted a finger. *They* didnae ken it wisnae a comet." He stared at D-CON bitterly, and shook his head. "Ah'll tell ye whit, though, ah wish it had've been."

After a few growls, the provost's car lurched off into the beginnings of the morning. Wisps of red had started to gather round the edges of the rooftops, and the unfathomable dark of the sky was about to break. As D-CON stood there, still gazing into the remnants of the night, Andy stared up at him.

"A hunner an ten kilometres a second? That's gey fast even for a comet, is it no?"

"IT IS."

Andy puffed his cheeks out thoughtfully.

"Jeez oh. Ah could see the point if it wis heading the ither wey. Ah've broke the sound barrier masel gittin oot o Galashiels." He smiled for a moment at the robot's unreflecting face, then let it drop. "Ach, no that Hawick's much better. But it's hame, eh? Ye ken everybody."

He paused as if conscious of having said the wrong thing, but D-CON showed no sign of having noticed. Andy let his hand rest on the monument's pedestal, tracing its inscription. It was too dark to read, and written in Latin, but he knew it off by heart. *From out of the depths it emerges, beautiful.*

"Do ... do ye never get hamesick yersel, sometimes?"

"NO. ALL THINGS MUST FIND A PURPOSE, AND I HAVE FOUND MINE ON EARTH. I SHALL BE AT HOME HERE, BEFORE LONG."

Andy instinctively patted the robot on its leg, somewhere about its knee. The metal was light and soft to the touch, like aluminium, and strangely warm.

"Ah went tae New York, wance," he said, "Thought aboot Hawick the hale time. Couple o hours on a plane an it felt like the ends o the earth. Ach, but the sights, man! Ken the Statue of Liberty?"

D-CON lifted up its arm, and its hand was blue with light.

"FROM HER BEACON-HAND GLOWS WORLD-WIDE WELCOME ..."

Andy smiled up into the lantern. Its beam was bright enough to shine the stars, but no-one else had chosen to see it. He shook his head.

"Never you mind, pal. You're daein alright. It's them buggers just need tae get used tae ye. But they'll get there, D-CON."

"B-CON."

"Eh?"

"MY NAME IS B-CON."

As Andy followed the robot's stare into the now starlit sky, a bat, suddenly visible against the gleam, fluttered past, and the air took on the pungent taste of lead. Never before had he witnessed skies so full of life, a horizon that brimmed with anything but streetlights and the cracks between curtains. Now, above the spire, three dots of light were developing slowly against the black, a perfect triangle that shimmered in the sky and hung there. He watched them coming, as if a fresh constellation was jostling into the order of things, a spearhead advancing through the aging cosmos.

He understood.

Beneath his palm, Andy felt the robot humming gently – happily, even. The stars were dying, and the news of some unfamiliar galaxy was finally reaching Earth.

Thomas Clark is a poet and writer. He is a regular columnist at The National. In 2015, he became Scottish football's first ever poet-in-residence with Selkirk FC. His most recent works include the poetry collection *Intae the Snaw* and the bestselling children's book *Diary o a Wimpy Wean*.
www.thomasjclark.co.uk

Published in *Shoreline of Infinity 5*

The Last Word

Ken MacLeod

One day | In the last year of the Obama Presidency | On the third day of the fourth month | Shortly after the bombardment of Damascus

the Teacher found by the roadside a fledgling fallen from its nest.

" 'Bad deeds vanish like the night,' " Trevithick read, pausing the app to check its latest output, " 'but good deeds shine forever like the day.' "

"That's not only bogus," I said. "It's a brazen and pernicious falsehood."

"Oh, sure," said Trevithick. "But that's not the point, is it? We have to submit it to the wisdom of crowds." He tapped Enter. The app resumed.

The wisdom of crowds, as measured by retweets and likes, left that meme to wither on the vine.

But if the online readership didn't like it, we had others. Thousands of them. Or rather, our app did. Later that app acquired other names. Back then, when we were two young coders running a shoe-string start-up out of a loft in a converted jam factory in one of the less fashionable parts of Kirkaldy, we called it Deepity Dawg.

Moved by compassion | In righteous wrath | Laughing heartily he | she picked it up and

fed it tenderly until it grew | placed it back in its nest | snapped its neck and

cast it in the bushes | fed it to a passing dog | roasted it

"Basically, it's a meme generator coupled with a learning algorithm," Trevithick explained. He refrained from explaining that the learning algorithm had been cobbled together for our final exam project. "It has a database trawled from" – he waved a hand vaguely – "old out-of-copyright texts, and a parser to combine tropes and phrases in ostensibly meaningful ways – sayings and stories. Most of them will be junk, of course. But it sends them all out as tweets or posts, records what response they get, and refines its model. Rinse and repeat. There's more to it than totting up retweets and likes – we have quality analyis built in, credibility metrics, etc. All the SEO and social marketing packages are off-the-shelf. Our USP is the learning algorithm. That's what we're bringing to the table, and what we can offer you a one-year exclusive on."

The Social Marketing Director of Smiles4Miles had been listening while scrolling through the detailed pitch on her tablet. She looked up, frowning.

"What's a *deepity*?" she asked.

"It's a term coined by Daniel Dennett," I said, "for something that's true but trivial, or profound but false. 'Love is just a word,' for example."

"Ah. I see."

"So," Trevithick went on, "the algorithm learns from the feedback to distinguish between what we call the three Ds – deep, deepity, or Dee –"

"Pack it in," the Social Marketing Director interrupted, with a chopping rapid motion of the hand. "We don't use that name around here."

Smiles4Miles was a fitness motivation company: it cluttered side shelves of high-street sportswear shops with its books, posters, videos, podcasts, apps, and apparel. The company now eyed the wider, and insatiable, spirituality and self-help markets. No wonder its directors wouldn't hear the biggest name in the woo business being bandied about.

"Bottom line," said the Social Marketing Director, "is that you think you can generate useful advice and inspiring quotes by natural selection?"

"Partly artificial," Trevithick admitted. "It takes a lot of tuning and pruning. But basically, yes."

I could almost see the Director's thinking. What we offered was potentially worth millions. What we asked in return was peanuts. Well, peanut and raisin energy bars, but you get the picture.

So did she. She gave us a year to come up with the goods.

Perplexed| Angered | Amused | Intrigued | Overjoyed | Tearfully

the followers asked: "Why have you done this?"

The Teacher answered:

After a close scrape when we (or rather, one of Deepity Dawg's online bot army of flying monkeys) attributed some inappropriate made-up quote to Mohammed, I hand-coded a fix to replace any accidentally-included names of real sages, prophets, messiahs, philosophers, rabbis, bodhisattvas and Zen masters with 'the Teacher'.

When bogus sayings, tales and homilies made up by other people, companies and bots began to be attributed to the Teacher, we knew we were on to something. When one of our original profundities turned up as the desktop wallpaper of a rival motivational company, Smiles4Miles didn't object, and nor did we. It was all grist to the algorithm's tirelessly churning mill.

The meme generator produced, of course, variant stories and sayings. Some worked, some didn't.

The algorithm learned.

The bird that the Teacher had | replaced in its nest | hand-fed for months

turned out to be a raven, which when fully grown

would eat nothing but seeds and nuts | attacked and carried off a young lamb | small child.

"Take a look at this," said Trevithick, half a year into the project. His tone was both amused and alarmed.

I scanned the discussion thread, drawn against my will into the raging debate.

"People are arguing about which sayings are *authentic*?"

"Looks like it," said Trevithick. He snorted. "Quite heatedly, and quite convincingly, too. They're almost swaying *me*."

"I know what you mean," I said. "I feel like jumping in and shouting, 'Look, you idiots, the Teacher would never have said something as stupid as *that*.'"

"Even though we both know he very well could."

"Uh-huh. 'He-stroke-she.' *It!* A thousand lines of code that *we* wrote."

"Have you looked through the best-of file recently?" Trevithick asked.

I nodded. "The sayings are definitely getting deeper."

He gave me an odd look. "Too deep, maybe."

I was about to reply when the phone rang. Trevithick picked it up. His answers became monosyllabic, his face stony. He rang off with a forced, false smile.

"Smiles4Miles is retrenching," he said. "Pulling back to the core business. And pulling the plug on us. We'll get the end-of-month payment, then that's that."

Numbed, I gazed out of the window across the rain-darkened Firth of Forth to the bright lights of Edinburgh's business district. Not for us, now. Not unless we found a different customer, and a different business model.

"Oh well," I said. "Like the Teacher says, we don't need hope to persevere."

"That wasn't the Teacher," said Trevithick. "It was – "

I pointed a finger at him. "Heretic!"

We both laughed, and hit the marketing sites.

The Teacher

slew it | praised it

saying:

We found another contract, with a social search agency. I made a copy of the code, amended it, and hooked it up to different data sources – the same learning algorithm could be adapted to brand recognition and reputation as well as to inspirational messaging. Leaving the earlier version running was less trouble than switching it off.

Six months later, a reminder popped up on my screen. I'd almost forgotten Smiles4Miles.

"Is that thing still running?" Trevithick asked. "The old Deepity Dawg?"

"I think so." I checked. "So it is. Might as well see what we've got."

I opened the best-of file, and began to read. Time passed unnoticed. I returned to the present with a jolt as Trevithick, quite unprecedentedly, shook my shoulder.

"Are you all right?" He sounded anxious.

I blinked at him. "I'm fine," I said. "Why do you ask?"

"You've been staring at the screen for ten minutes, with tears running down your face."

"What? Oh." I sniffed, blew my nose, shook my head. "No, there's nothing wrong. I got caught up in the text. It's incredible. Our app has written a... a revelation."

Trevithick snorted. "I don't believe you."

"Read it yourself."

He did. Sometimes he laughed, sometimes he frowned and nodded. After about an hour, his eyes too trickled tears. Eventually he pulled himself together.

"You're right," he said. "It's a revelation. Wiser than the *Meditations*, deeper than the *Gita*, subtler than the *Tao Te Ching*, earthier than *Proverbs*, more moving than the *Apology*... and all from the wisdom of crowds." He glowered at the server. "That thing, that thousand lines of code has learned to push all our buttons. What does that say about us? And it's not even an AI. It's just a learning algorithm with a library, Google Books, and Twitter."

"You know," I mused, "when you think what others have done with revelations so much less impressive..."

Trevithick laughed. "All our financial worries could be over for good!"

"And our real troubles just beginning," I pointed out. "As the Teacher said: 'If you meet the Teacher on the road, kill him!'"

"Or her," said Trevithick, as if by reflex.

"It," I reminded him.

We deleted all the files.

"The bird's fall was in the course of nature. Picking it up was a choice." | *"The consequences were bad, but was the deed not merciful?"* | *"Now at last the bird goes as nature intended."*

Ken MacLeod was born on the Isle of Lewis in 1954 and lives in Inverclyde. He has studied Zoology, researched biomechanics and worked in IT. He is the author of seventeen novels, from *The Star Fraction* (1995) to *The Corporation Wars: Emergence* (Orbit, 2017) and many articles, stories and poems.
His novels and stories have received three BSFA awards and three Prometheus Awards, and several have been short-listed for the Clarke and Hugo Awards.

Published in *Shoreline of Infinity 8½ -Edinburgh International Book Festival Edition*

Afterword: It's Funny Because it's True

Andrew J. Wilson

Once upon a time, it was just a joke: we told folk that *Shoreline of Infinity* was Scotland's best science-fiction magazine... Well, it was – by default. It was Scotland's only science-fiction magazine! Nevertheless, great material from all over the world was published in every issue. Then, in its third year of publication, several stories from the magazine were selected by Donna Scott for inclusion in NewCon Press's *Best of British Science Fiction 2017*, and editor Noel Chidwick took the prize for Best Magazine/Periodical at the 2018 British Fantasy Awards in Chester. The joke was funny because it was true.

While *Shoreline* is now more or less officially Scotland's best SF magazine, it wasn't the first. That was *Nebula Science Fiction*, which was published from 1952 to 1959. This was the passion project of Peter Hamilton (no, not the Peter Hamilton who wrote *The Night's Dawn Trilogy*, another one), a young Glaswegian who took advantage of spare capacity at the family business to print it. *Nebula* helped to launch the careers of Brian Aldiss, Harlan Ellison, Bob Shaw, Robert Silverberg and James White, among many others. Sadly, although Hamilton reported a world-wide circulation as high as 40,000 copies, limitations on foreign magazine imports in Australia and South Africa, and homegrown excise duties killed his brainchild when it was only seven years old.

After *Nebula* folded, it would be four long decades until a challenger appeared. This was *Spectrum SF*, edited by Paul Fraser, which ran for nine issues between 2000 and 2002. Another well-respected publication, it printed work by British SF greats Keith Roberts and John Christopher, and younger guns like Eric Brown and Charles Stross. Incidentally, both of the latter authors have graced the pages of *Shoreline*, and both now live in Scotland. Coincidence? Surely not! Unfortunately, history repeated itself, and once again, the cold economic equations killed *Spectrum SF*.

Thankfully, it was only thirteen years before co-founders Noel Chidwick and Mark Toner entered the fray and the *Shoreline* era began.

It should be noted that the gaps between magazines were plugged by a pair of anthologies. Duncan Lunan edited *Starfield: Science Fiction by Scottish Writers*, which was originally published by Orkney Press in 1989. Noel Chidwick's Shoreline of Infinity Publications/The New Curiosity Shop reprinted this seminal anthology last year. Neil Williamson and I co-edited *Nova Scotia: New Scottish Speculative Fiction*, which was published just in time for the Glasgow World Science Fiction Convention in 2005, and subsequently nominated for a World Fantasy Award. There are plans for Shoreline of Infinity to reprint *Nova Scotia* too.

So here we are, hurtling towards the end of another decade, and the *Shoreline* project goes from strength to strength. As I've noted, the magazine itself is winning well-earned recognition. Several books have now been issued by Shoreline of Infinity Publications/The New Curiosity Shop. The regular Event Horizon live shows are drawing enthusiastic crowds. A podcast called *Soundwave* has just been launched... And you hold in your hands *The Chosen from the First Age*, the editorial team's selection of their favourite stories from the first ten issues of the magazine. There are big names and newcomers, and an admirable diversity of contributors, who represent not only Scotland but the rest of the world. "The crème de la crème," as Miss Jean Brodie said in her prime.

I believe that the *Shoreline of Infinity* project can be summed up as Scotland reimagining itself and thinking about its future. Being a small country, that means listening to other voices, and considering our nation's place in the world and the universe.

I propose a Scottish toast to the good ship *Shoreline of Infinity*, and all who sail in her:

Here's tae us; wha's like us? Damn few – and they're a' deid!

The stories continue...

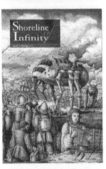

Come join us at the Shoreline of Infinity.
All issues, past, present and future available
from our website, in print or digital formats.
Subscriptions also available.

Use the special code:

shorelinechosen

for a 10% discount on your first order.

Shoreline of Infinity Science Fiction Magazine
www.shorelineofinfinity.com